SARATANI

A JAMES THOMAS NOVEL

BROOKE SIVENDRA

1

JAMES THOMAS

HART.
  Joshua Hart.

James's eyes were fixed to the screen, the name repeating over and over in his mind.

"Where did you get this?" James asked Samuel, wondering if he looked as ill as he felt.

Samuel drew in a deep, tension-filled breath. "From the CIA's database. I got an alert on Dasha, and when I logged in, this is what I found."

"I'm assuming Escanta is behind this, but how did they connect Joshua Hart with Liam Smith?"

Samuel nodded. "I don't know yet. Joshua Hart hasn't existed on paper for years—I made sure of that when I deleted his school reports, bank accounts, military records . . . No stone was left unturned, so my only explanation is someone is talking."

When James had crossed over into the CIA, his death had been staged. Joshua Hart died in battle, and James said goodbye to the life he'd known and everyone in it. If someone was talking, James thought it was most likely someone from the CIA.

"Do you think Dasha could've found out who you are?" Samuel asked.

"No," James said, returning his eyes to the image of her mutilated body. "I think they punished her because she told me how to find Escanta. That note is a message for me; they're trying to provoke me. They haven't been able to find me, so they're trying to draw me out."

James should've killed Dasha—he shouldn't have let her meet her end like that. He'd known she wouldn't be able to hide that shoulder wound, but he still hadn't killed her. Some delusional part of him thought she might survive, that she might be able to disappear before they found her, but he was wrong.

"I should've killed her, given her an easier death," James said quietly.

Samuel's lips turned down in a sympathetic frown.

James pinched the bridge of his nose. Hunting Escanta had to be his top priority because if they were able to find out he was Joshua Hart, there was only so long that James could hide in New York. They would eventually find him, and find Thomas Security. And then the lives of Samuel, Deacon, Cami, and Mak would be at risk.

Escanta had successfully provoked him, so they'd won on that account. And now he was going to hunt them relentlessly but carefully. He had to beat them at their own game and surprise them where they least expected him to show up.

In order to hunt down these men, he was going to have to leave Mak Ashwood in New York. She had just won two guilty verdicts and sent the head of the mob to prison for life. She had humiliated them, and for that there would be payback of some kind. He wasn't going to be able to protect her—he was going to have to trust his brother to do that while he fought the demons of his past on the other side of the world.

"Do we have any leads on Escanta other than the Docoss Hotel?" James asked.

Samuel sighed. "No, I told you these guys were careful. I've put together the list of associates from the hotel, but that's it—that's all I've found."

"Has Deacon confirmed when he'll be back?"

"Tomorrow, midday," Samuel said. "What are you going to do?"

James looked at his watch; it was nearing midday, so he had roughly twenty-four hours until his brother returned. But he didn't want to wait that long—he'd waited too long already. Samuel had been right: he should have followed up the Docoss lead as soon as they'd known about it.

Cami and the additional security team surrounding Mak were good—brilliant—but he needed Deacon here if he was going to be away. James mentally ran though the logistical possibilities for the next twenty-four hours, but there was only one real option in his mind. He was going to give Mak the same treatment he gave Jayce Thomatsu in Tokyo.

"Organize a jet to leave in a few hours. I'll go to London and have a chat with the manager of the Docoss Hotel, and we'll go from there," James said, drawing his phone from his pocket. He entered Cami's number.

She picked up on the second ring. "What's up?"

"Samuel's office," James said.

"Be there in two minutes," Cami said, the playfulness dropping from her voice.

James hung up and put his phone on the table.

"The jet is confirmed," Samuel said.

"Thanks," James responded, his eyes once more looking to the bloody pits where Dasha's eyes should've been. "When and where did they find her?"

"She was found two hours ago in a passageway not far from her apartment. There's not a lot of information coming through just yet; the CIA are no doubt scrambling to try and piece it together. If they find out Liam Smith paid her a visit, well, that's not going to be very good for us, is it?"

James looked over her injuries. "She wouldn't have talked to them. Look at the degree of mutilation, Samuel—Escanta had to do that in order to get her to talk. She didn't give up that information easily, and I would bet my life she kept her mouth shut until the end. Dasha was tough."

"I hope you're right," Samuel said.

The door swung open, and Cami took two steps into the room before her eyes bulged. James imagined he'd looked much the same.

"Oh my . . . that's Dasha, isn't it?" Cami asked.

"Correct. We're assuming Escanta got to her," James said.

She screwed up her nose like she'd smelled something rotten, and then her eyes darted between James and Samuel. "Who is Joshua Hart?"

"That's me," James said. "That's my birth name." Well, not really, but that wasn't a story he wanted to get into right now.

"*Joshua,*" she repeated, looking at him like she was seeing him for the first time. And then reality set in. "So how the hell did they find that out? This is very bad, isn't it?"

"Yes, it is. Samuel thinks it was leaked from the CIA, and I agree," James said. "And we've got a situation now because I need to leave and sort this out, and Deacon won't be back until tomorrow."

Cami's eyes widened. "I agree you need to sort this out, but are you really going to leave Mak with only me and the team to protect her?"

"Yes," James said, "because she's not going to leave this building until she needs to go to work on Monday morning."

Cami looked between James and Samuel again. "Well, I'm sure as fuck not going to be the one to tell her that."

A small smile crossed over Samuel's lips.

"I'll tell her," James said.

"Well, make sure your pistol's out of reach when you do," Cami said drily. "Deacon's not going to like this—he's not going to like you going on your own," she added.

"I know, but I need him here more than I need him beside me. I survived for a long time on my own, Cami, and I'll do it again," James said.

James had been thrust into a number of volatile situations as a single asset while he was in the CIA, and this trip would be no different. It was always better to have a friend watching your back, but on this occasion he'd have to make do without.

Cami pulled her lips to the side, her eyes filled with angst. "Damn . . . be careful, James."

"I will. I'm leaving in a few hours, so let's go over Mak's strategy for the next week. I want to make sure we're prepared for every possible situation, with my absence factored in."

The time passed quickly as they strategized, and re-strategized, over Mak's security plan. When he was as confident as he was going to get under the circumstances, he stood up. "Okay, I'm going to pack and then deliver the good news. Samuel, I'll see you in thirty minutes. Send everything to my laptop."

Samuel nodded his head, barely looking up from his computer.

The television welcomed James as he stepped into his apartment. He walked toward the noise, but when he reached his bedroom he was surprised to find Mak asleep. Her back was propped up on his pillows and her phone was in her hand like she had been reading it when she'd fallen asleep.

His eyes lingered on her, wanting nothing more than to crawl into bed with her. But, James could only hide for so long, and he would not let them find him in New York—he would not risk the lives of those he cared about. He'd find Escanta first and end this. He'd still have enemies, but Escanta was starting to make the Russians look like preschoolers.

James walked past the bed, ignoring his body's longing, and into his closet. He pulled out his black overnight bag and packed some clothes and retrieved his toiletries. He didn't need to pack anything else because his safe house in London had a supply of weaponry just for instances like this.

When his bag was packed he put it by the door.

"Mak," he said, sitting down on the edge of the bed.

She opened her sleepy eyes and looked around, surprised to see him. "I think I fell asleep," she said with a husky voice.

James smiled. "You did." She hadn't slept much over the past week, but she'd have plenty of time to catch up this weekend, because she wasn't going to be able to do much else.

"When did you get back? Is everything okay?" She crossed her legs beneath her and sat up.

"It will be okay, but I need to leave"—James looked at his watch—"in a few minutes. I'm going to be away for a little while."

"You're leaving? Now? What is going on?"

"I can't give you any details, Mak, you know that," James said gently.

She held his gaze, and he had that strange sensation again that she was tethering his mind, drawing information he didn't want to give her.

"I . . . well, how long will you be gone?"

"I don't know. A few days, maybe a few weeks," James said.

"Weeks?" She looked around the room and the pieces seemed to fall together. She looked at him with suspicious eyes. "Where is Deacon? When is he getting back?"

"Midday tomorrow."

Her eyes flared. "James," she said, "I am not staying here all weekend with nothing to do."

"There's lots to do here, and Cami will be with you."

"Cami is lovely, but I don't want to spend the weekend with her. I agreed to spend the weekend with you, and if that's not happening, then I'm going to spend it with my friends and family."

"You can't—"

"I can, and—"

"I told you there would be things you wouldn't like about your security, and this isn't even to do with us—this security measure is because of your own enemies. I've done the same thing to Jayce, I've done it to other clients, and I will do it to you if it means keeping you safe. This building is the safest place in the world for you, and you need to spend the weekend here. I would also like to be able to leave knowing you're safe."

"This is insane," she said bitterly.

"This is part of being a Thomas Security client," James said.

"It's becoming a very unappealing situation."

"I told you it would be," James said.

"Would you honestly be doing this if I was just a client? If there was nothing between us?" she asked.

"Yes," he said.

"I can't believe this," she said, looking away.

James checked his watch again—time was running out.

"Mak, I need to go. This isn't what I want—I don't want to leave—but I need to deal with this situation."

She stared him down. "Let me clarify, just to make sure we're on the same page: If I want to leave this weekend, I can't. You're essentially going to lock me up, and I can't leave even if I try. Is that what you're telling me?"

"Yes," James said. "This is life when the mafia is threatening to kill you. It's a temporary measure, Mak—it's not forever, at least not this level of security. Catch up on some sleep, reply to all of your messages and phone calls. If you want to work out, Cami can train you, and I promise it will be a much more efficient session than your barre class. And, before you know it, Monday morning will be here and you'll be back at work."

James saw the stubborn expression on her face and went on, "This is not me being overly paranoid: the risk to you is very high right now. You humiliated Bassetti and sent him to prison for life. You're a very intelligent woman; you know how these men operate. Do you really think they're not going to attempt to scare you for that? You came to us for a reason, and by winning the trial you increased the stakes of the game. Please, this weekend has nothing to do with us and everything to do with your own security situation. You're safe here, no one can touch you—take comfort in that."

"Can Maya and Kayla visit me at least?"

James considered it. They didn't normally have guests at Thomas

Security—the fewer people to see the inside of this building the better. Even with full security reports on both Mak's sister and her long-time friend, James was still hesitant.

"Maya can visit," James agreed.

"One win for me," she said with a small dose of attitude.

"A bigger win than you realize," James said.

Mak raised one eyebrow in apparent doubt.

"Let's go downstairs," James said. He turned off the television as Mak slipped on her shoes. James slung the strap of his bag over his shoulder and followed her downstairs to her apartment.

When she turned to face him, he took her hand, and drew her in. She didn't pull back, but she definitely wasn't jumping into his arms.

"We'll sort this security situation out, and things will get better—I promise. This is just one weekend," James said.

"And what if you're not back next weekend?"

"What happens next weekend completely depends on what happens this week. We'll see if the mafia tries anything, keep collecting intel, and go from there. I'll be overseeing everything regardless of where I am."

She pursed her lips, but James wasn't sure if it was an expression of anger or frustration. Or both.

"I'll call you when I can," James said quietly, wrapping her tiny body up in his arms.

She gave a small nod.

He leaned in to kiss her, and arousal flushed through his body as their lips connected. She parted her soft, tantalizing lips, and he deepened the kiss.

James let himself enjoy it, let himself revel in the moment, because if he couldn't find Escanta, if he couldn't fix this before it escalated, he had to walk away. He would not let Mak end up a mutilated corpse.

She slipped her hands under his sweater, her fingertips resting just above his jeans. Her touch tingled his skin, and he yearned to feel her hands all over him. But it wasn't in the cards today.

He pulled back, breathless, and cupped her cheek in the palm of his hand. His lips lingered on hers as he fought for the discipline to walk out the door and leave her.

When he knew he had not another minute to waste, he placed one last kiss on her lips. "I need to go," James whispered. "I'll talk to you soon."

He kissed her forehead, looked into her eyes, turned, and walked away.

Escanta didn't realize it, but they'd chosen the worst time to come after him, because for the first time in his life, James had someone worth fighting for. He had a life he was not prepared to walk away from; he had never been more motivated.

2

MAK ASHWOOD

Mak stood staring at the closed door. Earlier that morning they had negotiated the terms of their potential relationship, and a few hours later he was leaving with no explanation and no idea of when he might return. And she couldn't leave the building.

What was so urgent that he had to drop everything and leave? Was a client's life in danger? Was he walking into a dangerous situation? Would he get hurt? Would he return?

Mak rubbed her eyes. She knew she wasn't going to get the answers to any of her questions, and that frustrated her further. Was this the life she would have with him? He ran a high-risk business, and it wasn't unreasonable to assume this might happen often. Could she be in a relationship with someone who couldn't tell her what he was doing or where he was going? And with someone who couldn't promise he would return? Was that the life she wanted, even if it was with James Thomas?

Mak went into the kitchen and poured a glass of juice. She leaned back against the bench top, silently mulling over her thoughts.

When would she hear from him again? Would they be like the couples that spoke on the phone every day when one partner was away for work? Or would she not hear from him for a week? Or longer?

Mak didn't know; a relationship with James Thomas came with a lot of questions and few answers.

A knock at the door startled her and pulled her from her thoughts.

"Come in," Mak called out, and when the door opened Cami poked her head around it before she entered.

"Get your gym gear on," Cami said as she walked toward her.

Mak raised one eyebrow.

"It will be good for you; you can release some of the frustration bubbling in that little body of yours. And you've got nothing else to do anyway," Cami said, deadpan.

"Yes, I'm very well aware of that. I'm trying to work out how I'm going to spend the entire weekend in this apartment," Mak said.

"In this building," Cami corrected. "Come on, get changed and we'll kill an hour at least. And then I might even take you to do something fun."

"Like?"

"Can't say," Cami said, smiling. "You'll have to work out with me before I'll tell you."

Mak scoffed. "Good ol' bribery, huh?" She finished the last of her juice. "Give me a minute," she said, leaving Cami in the kitchen as she went to change.

She's right; I might as well do something. Sitting alone in the apartment with endless questions was a much less enticing option.

She rummaged through her bag, finding the only gym clothes she had. She needed someone to go to her actual apartment and pick up more clothes.

When she finished changing, she followed Cami to the gym. Mak had no idea where it was, but when they arrived a few floors down she noted the floor number, and slowly, as she was exposed to more of this building, she began to create a mental floor plan. The building seemed to have as many secrets as the Thomas brothers.

Mak was surprised to see they weren't alone in the gym. There were a handful of people already using the equipment.

"Thomas Security staff have access to the gym, twenty-four hours," Cami explained. "The staff generally work in shifts, so it's rare for this place to be empty. But it's also never crazy busy either—we all have very different schedules."

Cami retrieved two towels from a cupboard and two bottles of water from the refrigerator then led Mak to the treadmills. Mak stepped up onto the sides, and Cami did the same on the machine next to her.

"We'll start with a short run. Let's walk for a few minutes, then we'll increase the speed," Cami said, showing Mak how to use the machine. When they started walking, Mak looked over the gym—like their theatre room, the Thomas brothers hadn't spared any expense in this room. Or any room of the building, as far as she'd been able to ascertain.

The first few minutes passed easily, but when Cami increased the speed, Mak realized how tough this workout was going to be. She was relatively fit but guessed Cami was planning to push her limits.

Twenty minutes later, Cami decreased the speed of Mak's treadmill and smiled slyly. "Warm?"

"Please don't kill me today," Mak said breathlessly.

"Define kill, exactly," Cami said, laughing. "Okay, now the fun starts."

They moved to the weights area and before long Mak's legs were burning. Cami was relentless, and after a grueling hour of sweating, cursing, and fighting to breathe through sequences of squats and jumps, Mak thought she might pass out.

"Good work," Cami said, patting Mak's back.

Mak rested her hands on her knees and looked at the floor. Did James really want her to do an hour of this every day? *Holy crap!*

"It gets easier," Cami said, rolling out a yoga mat. "Sit down; let's stretch."

They stretched for the next fifteen minutes, Mak's favorite part of the workout. It also gave her an opportunity to assess their gym companions. There was not an ounce of fat on anyone; they all looked strong.

"Is it a requirement for Thomas Security staff to work out a certain number of hours per week?" Mak asked quietly.

"Not exactly," Cami said, "but we do need to pass monthly physical tests, so our trainers will work with us and advise if we need to increase our time in the gym. To be honest, though, in this industry exercise becomes as much about the mental benefits as it does the physical. It can be a very stressful job, and working out helps offset that."

"I can imagine," Mak said. "How are you always so relaxed, though?" Cami was her primary bodyguard, and therefore Mak's safety must weigh heavily on her shoulders.

"I'm not always, but in this field you do get accustomed to certain levels of stress. It's definitely not a job for everyone—it takes a certain mentality to deal with the pressure of protecting someone's life."

Mak's body was still trembling from the workout, but her curiosity for the next item on Cami's agenda was mounting. "So, have I earned the privilege of finding out what we're doing next?"

Cami winked. "Now the fun really begins." She stood up and held out her hand, helping Mak onto her wobbly legs.

They threw their towels into the laundry basket on the way out and walked toward the elevator. They took it down to B2 and stepped out into an empty hallway lined with doors. Cami turned to the right, and Mak followed, but not before she had a good look down the long hallway.

"What's that way?" Mak asked, looking over her shoulder.

"*Secrets*," Cami said, laughing.

Mak looked at her, waiting for Cami to elaborate, but she didn't. Instead, Cami entered a code at a single door and opened it to reveal what looked to be a shooting range.

Mak looked around and then eyed Cami suspiciously. What exactly had James told her about the terms and conditions of their relationship?

"What?" Cami asked, her eyes darting from side to side.

"Why did you bring me here?"

"Because it's fun, and I assume it's something you haven't done before," Cami said. "Why do you think I brought you here?"

"Because James told you to," Mak said, crossing her arms.

Cami thought about it for a minute. "Honestly, I don't really know what is going on between the two of you. The first time he admitted anything was even going on was this morning. If James wants you to learn to shoot, which I'm assuming he does from your comment, he hasn't told me. However, I've worked with him long enough to know that's what he would want. Let's be honest, you have no hope of fighting me off, let alone someone like James, so weapons will be your best bet. But that's not why we're here. It is fun, and I also need to practice, so we'll do it together."

Mak eyeballed her, but like James, Cami's face never gave away anything. "Okay," Mak said, looking around. She had no idea what to do, and her heart was beating a little faster. She'd never held a gun in her life.

"Good," Cami said. "I'll be back in a minute." She entered a code to another door and disappeared behind it.

While Mak waited for her to come back, assuming she wasn't supposed to see whatever was behind that door, she took full stock of the shooting range. It was long, and there were fifteen targets hanging at the end, side by side. The targets appeared to be a piece of black cardboard with a white outline of a torso and head, and then an internal grid.

Could Mak really shoot someone if she had to? Maybe she could shoot them in the arm, or the leg, rather than kill them. *I could do that . . . I think.*

Cami came back into the room with a two pairs of ear-muffs, glasses, and two guns. "Have you ever fired a gun?"

"Never in my life," Mak mumbled. Cami handed her the gun, and she held it awkwardly. *What do I do with it?*

She didn't have to wait long for any instructions, and before she knew it Cami had her standing at the bench with the pistol aimed at a target. Mak's heart thumped in her ears as she fired the first shot.

"Good. Shoot five more slow rounds," Cami said.

Mak took a deep breath, and focused on the technique Cami had shown her. But she shifted her aim, going for the shoulder. Not a single bullet hit her intended target.

Cami stared at the target. "What exactly are you aiming for?"

"The shoulder," Mak said, carefully putting her pistol down on the bench so it didn't accidentally go off—if it could do that.

Cami pressed a button that moved the target closer to them. She looked it over for a moment. "Why?"

"I'm trying to hurt my target, not kill it," Mak said, crossing her arms over her chest.

Cami rubbed her lips together. "What if someone is trying to kill you?"

"Then I'll shoot them in the shoulder and run," Mak said.

"First, never turn your back on someone who is trying to kill you. And second, even if you shoot them in the shoulder, it might not be enough to stop them. And you might not get another chance." She was very unapologetic about her stance.

"I'll take my chances," Mak said, matching Cami's resolution.

"You might think differently if you ever, God forbid, end up in that situation. Now, even if you're going to aim for the shoulder, you've got some serious practice to do," Cami said.

Mak rolled her eyes—James was right about her: she certainly loved to tell the truth.

Mak didn't pick up the gun again, though, opting to watch Cami instead. Cami went straight for the target's forehead, and if it were a real person, their brains would've exploded out of their head with the impact of that bullet—Cami was a good shot.

"Lots of practice and two tough bosses who insist on perfection. Well, as close to perfection as possible," she said, not taking her eye off the target.

"Why are you aiming for the head and not the chest?" Mak asked. If Cami's intent was to kill, wouldn't it be easier to go straight for center mass?

"The preferable shot is the chest—always—but sometimes you

aren't given that option, like in a hostage situation, and so I need to practice both."

It made Mak uncomfortable to think of James or Deacon as being killers, but it felt even worse to think of Cami as being one.

Cami's past seemed to be as protected as the brothers', and Mak wondered what events had led her to the career she had—and one she obviously loved. In the weeks they had known each other, Mak had never seen her look tired, or stressed, or ever heard her complain about anything. In fact, she always seemed to be in a good mood. She appeared to really enjoy her life, and Mak thought that was rare in a world where a lot of people were dissatisfied with theirs.

"That gun isn't going to shoot itself," Cami said.

Mak rolled her eyes but picked it up. She hoped she would never have to use a gun, but if there was one thing Mak was, it was competitive, and she hated to be bad at anything. She looked at the gun now as a challenge, something she wanted to master. She was going to be a perfect shot—in the shoulder.

Cami's instructions silently reeled through her mind as she focused on the task. She pulled the trigger over and over until it was empty.

Cami looked at her with a sly grin. She put her weapon down but didn't say anything. Cami showed her how to reload the pistol, and then they went back to the benches to destroy their targets. Mak improved with every bullet, but she still had a long way to go.

"I think that's enough for one day," Cami said.

"I'm just warming up!"

"Okay, crazy, put the gun down," Cami said, laughing. "In all seriousness, you did improve. We won't tell James about those first few shots, though, or that you're still aiming to wound," she said, rolling her eyes and taking Mak's pistol.

Cami started to walk away but turned back with a mischievous smile on her lips. "While we're in the habit of keeping secrets from James, do you want to see something?"

Mak nodded rapidly.

"Come with me," Cami said, walking toward the locked door.

Mak followed her like a puppy dog following its owner.

Cami opened it, and held the door wide for Mak.

Mak's eyes doubled in size as she looked at the large room. It was three times the size she had assumed it would be based on the range dimensions, and every wall was loaded with weaponry. Mak looked around in awe. Was Thomas Security preparing for a war?

3

JAMES THOMAS

A distracted mind was a dangerous mind. It made errors, and those errors had consequences. And speaking with Mak Ashwood would only distract him. James had landed in London an hour ago, and his driver had pulled up three blocks from his safe house. As he walked the rest of the way, he was in battle mode. He was the old James Thomas, the one who loved to get himself into the thick of a situation and get out again. The one who was violent, who enjoyed punishing those who deserved it. And he hoped his next victim was going to be one of those.

James had an appointment with Brian Roberts, the manager of the Docoss Hotel, in two hours. Samuel had identified the Docoss Hotel as a favorite of the Escanta boys, but the question was: *Why*? Why did they stay there? There were thousands of hotels in London, but several of them had stayed at the Docoss. It wasn't a coincidence, because coincidence was a term people used when they didn't know why certain events aligned. No, there was a reason the Escanta boys stayed there, and James Thomas was not leaving until he knew what it was.

James let himself into the basement apartment he had purchased six years ago. Safe houses were a safety measure, and they now had nine across the globe. Only four people knew their locations. Not too long ago, James had revealed the Tokyo apartment to Jayce Tohmatsu, but James had since sold it and relocated to another building—protecting it. He doubted Jayce would ever be a threat, but James trusted almost no one.

He took a bottle of water from the refrigerator and went straight into the guest bedroom. He pushed the bed to the side of the room and rolled up the floor rug, exposing a trap door. He entered the code to unlock it and then hinged open the door, exposing a cavity they'd cut into the basement floor. In it were his favorite toys. He already had a pistol in his bag but he took out another one, as well as three knives, a scalpel, and a pair of pliers. It was the perfect combination of weapons—easy to conceal, but capable of delivering an unimaginable brutal experience. He closed the trap door, put the furniture back in place, and took his weapons into the kitchen. He cleaned both pistols and reloaded them, then secured the weapons to his body. He changed into the spare suit hanging in the wardrobe. In addition to a supply of weaponry, their safe houses were also stocked with clothing.

James finished his bottle of water, and then retrieved his earpiece from his bag and put it in place.

"Samuel," James said, testing the communication device.

"Copy."

"I'm set. I'm going over to the Docoss Hotel now," James said.

"Good luck."

James locked the door behind him and went to the car park where his car was waiting for him. It was part of the fleet of custom armored cars they owned, and every safe house had one.

He turned the ignition on, but didn't bother to set the navigation system—he knew exactly where he was going. The streets were busy, but James didn't let the traffic frustrate him. He was in no particular hurry, although he was eager for his appointment—an appointment Brian knew nothing about, and an appointment Brian was not likely to enjoy. James's favorite kind of appointment.

He had a stroke of luck that Brian hadn't disappeared since

James's Hungary trip and subsequent dismembering of Escanta. But Escanta, or the men in the next layer, had no idea he would go to the Docoss Hotel—why would they? Only Samuel would be able to find a link like that; James would've never found it on his own—not without months, or years, of surveillance. Samuel was a godsend, and someone James needed to protect at all costs. Not only because of his skill set, which was very impressive, but also because he was family.

James patiently veered in and out of the traffic until he pulled into a park around the corner from the Docoss. The sun was rising as James exited the car and walked toward the hotel. Mr. Roberts was a man of routine, and he arrived at the hotel at five in the morning, every morning, where he drank two cups of coffee and caught up on paperwork in his office. James knew this because Samuel's monitoring team had been watching Mr. Roberts's every move for the past few weeks—via the Docoss Hotel's surveillance system.

The doorman held the intricate gold doors of the Docoss Hotel open, and James walked through without a second look. He carried his briefcase, which contained only his second pistol. James had memorized the floor plan on the flight over, so he knew exactly where to go. He walked past the concierge toward the elevator, and when he was out of sight of the front-desk staff, he turned again and walked toward the exit stairwell. Mr. Roberts's office was on the twenty-fourth floor, which would be locked from the stairwell—but James had a plan for that. He took the stairs two at time, climbing all twenty-four floors without stopping. Adrenaline was fueling his already fit body, and he didn't need to stop to catch his breath, even when he reached the top. And as he'd assumed, the door was locked. James pulled the scalpel from its holster and jimmied the manual lock. It would blunt the scalpel a little, but that would only make it more painful for Mr. Roberts—if James had to use it.

James listened carefully, and using the slightest of touch, wiggled the scalpel until he felt the sweet spot and it unlocked. Using his fingertips, he pushed the door ajar, just enough to survey the hallway. It was quiet and empty. He silently closed the door behind him and stalked toward Mr. Roberts's indulgently luxurious office. It took up a good portion of the floor, which was a mistake for Roberts because it meant fewer witnesses. His assistant wasn't scheduled to start work for another forty-five minutes, and James would be long gone by then —with or without Mr. Roberts.

James kept his breath even as he neared the office. He stopped, listening for a moment. The office was silent, other than an occasional rustling of papers. James drew his pistol and seized the opportunity.

With the weapon pointed at Mr. Roberts's forehead and his index finger over his lips, James let himself in and closed the door behind him. James watched like a predator stalked their prey—he noted every detail: his change in breathing, where his eyes were darting, the beads of sweat forming along his hairline, the color of his pallor transitioning to a greenish-white.

"W-who are you?" Mr. Roberts asked, forcing the words out.

"That is none of your concern. I'm going to ask you a series of questions, and you're going to answer them because I know where you live—with your wife and two sweet daughters—and if I find out you have lied to me, the next time you see me will be in your family kitchen. Now, put your palms flat on the desk," James instructed.

Mr. Roberts did, but slower than James would've liked. James raised one eyebrow and Mr. Roberts drew a shaky breath.

"This can be quick and easy, or long and *very* painful. Understood?"

Mr. Roberts swallowed like he had an apple stuck in his throat. "I don't know what you could possibly want."

James smiled. "I think you do. I want to know all about the Escanta boys, and why they enjoy staying at your hotel, Mr. Roberts."

His face was now a ghostly green. "*Escanta*? I don't know who or what you're talking about," he stammered.

"Yes, you do," James said, testing him.

"I swear, I have no idea what you're talking about."

James paused. "We can either talk about this now, or we can talk about it in your kitchen while your wife bleeds to death before your eyes. Which would you prefer?"

Mr. Roberts's chest heaved. "Please, I don't know. I really don't know," he said with a voice tight with panic.

James drew out his scalpel with his free hand and twirled it in front of his eyes.

Mr. Roberts looked at James pleadingly. "This is crazy," he said, looking around. "Please, I swear, I don't know."

Only when the man was on the verge of tears did James concede that perhaps he didn't know. But that didn't mean he couldn't find out. James kept his pistol pressed against the manager's temple.

"I'm going to take a chance and say I believe you. But remember the consequences if I find out you've lied to me," James said, looking at him. "I want you to look up three names."

James told him the first name, and Mr. Roberts quickly typed it into the reservations database. When the file loaded he appeared to look over it and then blankly looked back at James. James didn't need to read the file—it was already on his laptop.

"Anything about this man seem familiar to you?" James asked.

Mr. Roberts turned back to the computer screen, looked over it again, and shook his head.

James gave him the next name, and they repeated the process. Again Mr. Roberts shook his head, and James felt a surge of frustration bubbling in his chest.

Once the third file had loaded, Mr. Roberts shook his head once more but then stopped. "Wait," he said, and reloaded the previous files.

"Well, nothing seems familiar about the men, but the dates they checked in all coincide with"—he cleared his throat—"the parties we hold."

"Parties?" James repeated.

"Well, a party of sorts. They are held once per month. An underground gathering of London's elite who have a little . . . wild side, shall we say?"

"Keep talking," James instructed.

"They are," Mr. Roberts said, lowering his voice as if someone might overhear, "sex parties, basically. Sex, drugs, loud music. They are held off-site in a warehouse, but entry is limited only to those staying in this hotel. It's very exclusive, which is part of the appeal, amongst others things—obviously."

"When is the next one scheduled?"

"In two weeks, on the twenty-eighth," Mr. Roberts said.

This news displeased James—he didn't want to wait two weeks for another lead.

"I want my name at the door, and I will not be making a reservation. Make sure the name *Anthony Carter* is on the list. And if I bring any guests with me, they will all be granted access—no questions asked—without weapon checks. Understood?"

Mr. Roberts nodded his head.

"Listen to me very carefully. These men have no reason to suspect I found out about this party via you, and you should remember that. Your involvement in this is finished, provided you haven't lied to me.

"If, however, I find out you have, or you alert anyone to my visit, you will find yourself living in hell. Don't think I'm bluffing about killing your family—I'm not. I've done it before and I will do it again if need be," James said, pressing his pistol hard against the man's temple.

Mr. Roberts squeezed his eyes shut and screwed up his face like he was waiting for the trigger to be pulled. But James didn't pull it— not on that occasion—because the man didn't deserve it. At least not yet.

"Keep your mouth shut," James said, keeping his eyes on Mr. Roberts as he backed away from him and exited the office. James moved swiftly, leaving the same way he entered, and he emerged onto the street without incident.

Two weeks.

"Samuel," James said as he walked back to his car.

"Copy. I've set up a code to track every reservation for that night. I'm not sure what more we can do at this point."

James agreed. He thanked Samuel and then turned off his earpiece as he pulled into traffic. Without another lead, it was pointless to stay, especially with the risk of Mak's situation in New York.

But he would stay a few days regardless, just to watch Mr. Roberts—if he was going to talk, he'd do it sooner rather than later. And who knew—maybe Mr. Roberts would draw the Escantas out of wherever they were hiding.

James drove away from the Docoss Hotel toward his safe house, but he didn't go directly home. He couldn't see a tail, but he wasn't taking any chances. He went to a familiar restaurant two suburbs over to fuel his body and make a phone call.

4

MAK ASHWOOD

Mak's phone rang, pulling her from slumber. She looked at her flashing cell phone on the bedside table. Who was calling so early? She rolled over, reached for it, and when she saw the caller ID she smiled—he was worth being woken up for.

"Hello," she said with a husky voice, and then winced as her abdominal muscles screamed when she propped herself up against the cushions.

"Hey. How are you doing?" James asked.

"Well, I can hardly move because Cami destroyed me in the gym yesterday, but other than that I'm fine. How are you? How is the *situation*?"

"I told you she'd give you a good workout," James said. "The *situation* is manageable—at present. I need to follow up on some items over the next few days, but I should be home by Wednesday, provided nothing changes."

"Right," Mak said. There were so many questions she wanted to ask him, but she knew it was pointless. "Are you okay?"

"Me?" James sounded surprised. "Yes, I'm fine. I'm grabbing some food and thought I'd give you a call. What else did you do yesterday?"

Mak wondered if he knew already and was being polite, or if he honestly had no idea. "Post workout, Cami treated me to some time in your shooting range," Mak said, biting her lip. She left out her exploration of the weapons room. When Mak had reached for the AK-47 Cami had been quick to stop her.

"You did?" James asked, and Mak thought he was smiling. "How did it go?"

"I'm a brilliant shot," Mak said, grinning.

James laughed. "Are you lying to me, Mak? I'm going to check with Cami, and believe me, she'll give you up and throw you under the bus." His gentle threat was loaded with seduction.

"Well, it was my first time, so of course there's room for improvement. But you better be careful, Thomas, I might end up a better shot than you."

James scoffed. "Not a chance."

"You never know."

"I know. And I have years of experience on you. I do like this competitive motivation, though," James said.

"Well, I like to excel at everything I do, so I don't see why shooting a pistol should be any different."

"Oh, I agree. The better shot you are the happier I will be," James said, bringing out the elephant in the room. Mak still hadn't agreed to his relationship terms and conditions, and if she couldn't, there would be no relationship at all.

"Did you speak with Maya? Is she coming over?" James asked, changing the subject, and Mak wondered if his thoughts had drifted in a similar way.

"Yes, she's going to bring brunch over and stay for a few hours. She's quite excited, I think. The fact that your entire life is cloaked in secrecy only makes it more intriguing for people; it makes them ask more questions."

"True," James said. "But there isn't another option, particularly if our acquaintances want to live a long, healthy life." His voice was void of any humor.

Mak was quiet for a moment. "I'm struggling with that, with not knowing anything about you, or even where you are. I don't know what kind of situation you're in, but there is a chance you might not come home, right? If something happened to you, I mean."

"Mak, I've told you more about myself than I've told most," James said. "I know it's hard, but I'm keeping my life private to protect you, that's all. And, yes, there is a chance something could happen to me; but I'm very careful, very calculated . . . and I'm very good at what I do. I've survived in this field for a long time, but there is always a risk that something goes wrong and I get hurt. I can't make you any promises, and I'll never be able to."

Mak sighed, and then changed the subject again as the conversation was going nowhere. "So, which brother is better at Ping-Pong?"

James chuckled. "I would say I am, but Deacon would likely disagree. You should play him today, but I'm warning you, he has very fast reflexes. You might lose, Mak."

Mak could imagine that sexy smirk on his lips. "You really have to stop underestimating me."

James barked out a laugh. "We'll see. It's not a bad thing to be underestimated, though."

"On that we actually agree," Mak said, stifling a yawn.

"Did you not sleep well?"

Mak shook her head. "I slept fine, I'm just drained after the trial. I'm always like this when a big trial finishes. I feel like I pour everything into it, and by the end I'm just exhausted. Give me a week, though, and I'll be fine."

"Fine, physically," James said. "But how are you feeling about the third verdict?"

Kate's verdict—the one that came back not guilty. *I should've won.* "The same, and that's not going to change anytime soon."

"Two out of three is pretty good, Mak," James said. "You did your job, and you did it extremely well. You can feel bad about that third verdict, but you should also be proud of the two verdicts that will put him behind bars for the rest of his life."

"I know," Mak mumbled, sinking into the bed a little. She wished he were in New York, in bed with her, wrapping her up in his strong arms. For a man who she concluded—from the scattered pieces she'd been able to put together—could be quite dangerous, everything about him comforted her. Which was ironic, given her first impression of him.

"Any updates on this mafia situation?" Mak asked. She felt like she was being kept in the dark about that as well.

"No, not yet. I'm going to call Samuel when we hang up, but if anything important had come up he would've contacted me. Keeping you safe in Thomas Security serves its purpose, but it also makes it difficult to garner any more intelligence because they can't try anything, and therefore we can't intercept them at any point. When you go to work tomorrow, we'll need to be very careful because they may be getting impatient. You don't need to do anything, though, and you should try not to worry about this. My team knows what to do, and I'll be back in a few days. We'll sort this out, and it's in all of our best interests if that's sooner rather than later."

Mak nodded in response. "Okay."

"I should really check in with Samuel now because I have to look over a few things soon."

"Sure," Mak said. "I'm glad you called."

"Me too. I'll call again when I can," James said and hung up.

It was a phone call that left her with mixed emotions, much like their unofficial relationship. She wanted to say yes, to agree to everything, but she wasn't that kind of girl. And she never would be.

Mak pulled the comforter up under her chin and curled her legs to her chest. She closed her eyes, preparing to catch a few more hours of sleep before Maya arrived with brunch.

Once again Mak's phone pulled her from her sleep, but this time she was surprised to see it was her mother.

"Mom?"

"Mak . . ." Her voice cracked as she said her daughter's name.

Mak's pulse accelerated like a speeding car. "Mom? What's wrong?"

"I . . . I just . . ." She let out a whimper like she was holding back tears. "Mak, where are you?"

"I'm in the apartment, in the security building. Tell me what's going on." Mak felt the fear rise in her chest.

"I'm so sorry, Mak, I don't know how to tell you this . . ."

Someone died. Dad died. Every horrible possible situation ran through Mak's mind.

"I was just vacuuming," Mak's mother continued, "and as I pushed it under the kitchen buffet something got stuck in the head of the cleaner. It made a loud, rattling noise, and when I turned it off and dismantled it . . . I found a ring." She let out a shaky breath.

Mak frowned. *A ring?*

"It's Eric's ring, Mak. It's silver, and it has the inscription, 'Forever and Always'—it has to be his."

Mak felt the air catch in her throat. "Mom . . ." Mak quickly tried to think back over the months before Eric's disappearance. When had they last been at her parents' house? She couldn't remember, but they hadn't gone there often—they were always too busy working, and her parents usually came to the city to visit them and their four other children who lived in Manhattan.

"I don't understand," Mak's mom continued. "It's been so long, and I vacuum under this buffet every week. How did I not find it before?"

How was that possible?

"I mean," Mak's mother continued, "I guess it could've been pushed around, and not actually suctioned up," she said without confidence. "But why would it be in our home? I can't remember when he was here last. I can't remember . . . Gosh, it was so long ago. I need to sit down."

"Mom, where is the ring now?" Mak asked.

"I'm holding it—I can't stop looking at it."

"Put it down on the buffet," Mak said quickly. Her job as criminal prosecutor had taught her enough about evidence to know it shouldn't be tampered with. There was nothing to suggest a sinister reason as to why the ring would be in her parent's home, but still, Mak knew it should be tested by forensics. *Had he been wearing his ring in the weeks leading up to his death?* Again Mak couldn't remember, but she didn't recall him not wearing it, which she thought she would've.

"Don't touch it again, Mom. Just leave it there until I can organize . . . someone to collect it. I want to have it tested," Mak said.

"For what? It's his, Mak, it can't be anyone else's."

"I know, but it could have someone's fingerprints on it. Or . . . I don't know, I just think it should be tested. I can't figure out how it's ended up in your home, or how you haven't found it before. That's strange, don't you think?"

"Yes, I suppose so . . . I think I'm in shock. I can't take my eyes off it. It's like a sign from the dead, don't you think?"

Mak raised an eyebrow. "I don't know what to think." Mak knew that was an understatement. "Mom, I'm going to make a call and then I'll call you back, okay? Don't touch the ring again, though, just leave it on the buffet until I call you back."

It was possible her mother had already unintentionally destroyed any evidence on the ring, but she still had to find out.

She hung up and called the one person who would be most likely to find the answers, and the one she also didn't particularly want to discuss her husband with.

He picked up immediately. "Hi, Mak."

"James, I just got a call from my mother and—"

"I know, my monitoring team alerted Samuel and connected us in on the call. I've got a car departing for your parents' house now to pick up the ring and do some surveillance."

Mak blinked. She knew Thomas Security's people were efficient, but that was remarkable.

"What do you think about it?" Mak asked, but didn't wait for an answer; she began verbalizing the rambling thoughts in her mind. "I don't remember him not wearing the ring. I can't remember the last time we were there together . . . I just can't remember."

James paused. "Tell me what the buffet in your parents' home looks like."

"It's a wooden cabinet, Scandinavian kind of style, along a wall in the kitchen. Why?"

"How often does your mother vacuum?"

Mak stilled, realizing the conclusion he'd also come to. "What are you saying?"

"I think it's unlikely the ring has been sitting there all this time," James said carefully.

"Do you think it was put there? Someone has been in my parents' home? Oh my God," Mak said, pressing her palm against her forehead.

"I'm not saying that just yet, and you don't need to worry because we're leaving a security team there with them until further notice. But, unless it's somehow fallen off the back of the cabinet or something, I think it's impossible that your mother has not once managed to vacuum that ring up in the past thirteen years. It was a good idea to tell her to put it down; we'll run full forensics on it, which should tell us a lot. It's silver, so if it's been sitting there unnoticed for years, it should be appropriately tarnished, et cetera.

"It's strange," James continued, "but not necessarily alarming at this stage. The boys will be there soon and Samuel has already started going through some data to see if he can find anything."

"Thank you," Mak said, bewildered by the situation they had found themselves in. "When will you have the forensics results?"

"Later today. I'll keep you updated. What time is Maya coming over?" James asked.

"In a few hours," Mak responded, but her mind was still on the ring.

"Good," James said. "Keep busy today, Mak, and try not to think about it too much. I'll let you know when results come back from forensics."

"Thanks, James," Mak said to her potential boyfriend now investigating her missing husband's wedding ring. *What a situation.*

"You're welcome, but you don't need to thank me," he said before hanging up.

Mak went into the kitchen for a glass of water to moisten her desert-dry throat. As she drank, she absentmindedly looked over the maze of skyscrapers.

Is the ring a sign from the dead?

Or is it something else completely?

5

JAMES THOMAS

James twirled his cell phone in his hand, waiting for Samuel to call. He didn't have to wait long.

"Where are the boys?" James asked, noting the time on his watch.

"They're about thirty minutes from Mak's parents' house. We're looking through all available CCTV footage of the area, as well as phone records, transport systems—everything. So far, nothing has turned up. I don't know what to think about this," Samuel said.

James didn't either, but he knew he didn't like it.

"That ring hasn't been sitting there all this time, Samuel, no fucking way—she would've found it before now."

"I agree, but at this point we don't have evidence to even give an inkling otherwise. It's very, very strange," Samuel agreed.

Too strange. And the gut instinct he relied on, that almost never let him down, seemed to agree with him. All along, James felt like they were missing something, and he was even more certain of that now. The problem was backing up his gut feeling with intel.

James blew out a frustrated breath. "Keep me updated. I want to know for sure that this guy's dead, Samuel."

"I don't think it's safe to assume he is until proven otherwise. I'll keep you posted," Samuel said, ending the call.

What were you up to, Eric? Or, what are you up to? If you're alive, why haven't you touched the money in your offshore accounts? If Eric was alive, he'd done a fine job at disappearing and leaving no clues behind. Which meant he had help—expert help—help at that level would be able to move money into his hands, making it look like it went back into the dirty hands that paid it. The fact that it hadn't moved had always been a concern for James. It neither confirmed nor ruled out his death, but what it did was highlight the shit he was deep in: Eric had been playing with some bad boys.

And Mak truly seemed to have no idea of the lies he'd told and the double life Eric had lived. James could only assume she'd not paid much attention, because she was too observant not to catch him on a single lie unless she wasn't looking. And if she hadn't been paying attention, it was possible he hadn't been wearing his ring in the weeks, or even months, prior to his disappearance. The ring could've fallen out of something Mak's mother had moved and somehow ended up underneath that cabinet. James couldn't rule out the ring not having been in that house for the past thirteen years, but he was almost positive it hadn't.

It would be a couple of hours before forensics had the results, and with a team protecting Mak's parents, there wasn't much more that could be done at this stage, so James drew his attention back to his own situation—one that was also at a temporary standstill.

Another incoming call sent his cell into a vibrating frenzy again.

"Samuel," James said.

"We have a bit of a situation here," Samuel said. "This has nothing to do with that ring. I was just looking at the reservation list for the Docoss Hotel's party, which requires photo identification, and I recognized one of them. The CIA was hunting him at one stage; at that time he was using the alias Troy Taylor. Basically, he is an asset gone wrong—a bit like you. He decided to go out on his own, and he caused a hell of a mess. I'm pulling all his files from the CIA database and sending them to you. I'll spend more time looking at it this afternoon, but I'm caught up in this ring situation at the moment. I'll get back to you."

"Thanks," James said, then hung up and opened the email program on his phone—waiting for the files to arrive. He was still impatiently watching it when something, or rather someone, caught his attention. In his peripheral vision he saw a familiar face, one he had not seen for years.

James held his position, seeming to be casually distracted by his phone, and didn't react—but his attention was on the man walking past him. The man continued on, showing no indication he had recognized James, but James wasn't prepared to take any chances. When the man was fifty feet in front of him, James dropped money onto the table to pay for his breakfast and stood, moving toward the lurking shadows of the buildings.

It had been some time since he'd incidentally seen someone from his past. A few men, intentionally hunting him, had found him. And there were the others he'd sought out; but it was certainly unusual for an old acquaintance to stroll by the café he was eating breakfast at on a short trip to London.

James looked into the glass windows of the shop fronts as he walked, observing the reflections of the people in them. He didn't have a sense he was being watched, but he could never be too careful —certainly not in this game.

He'd never worked with this man, but they had run in the same circles for a few years. The man knew him as Liam Smith, as most did, even though James must have assumed more than a hundred aliases during his years with the CIA.

His acquaintance entered a store ahead and James fell farther behind. James stopped and drew his phone from his pocket, looking like most of the street's patrons: heads down, attention absorbed by the cell phone in their hands, walking blindly ahead. He lifted his eyes to scour the street for a waiting spot, one that would hide him without drawing attention. And one that wasn't visible from the shop the man had entered. James noted the time, monitoring how long the man spent inside.

Across the street was a small café, and the smell of strong coffee and baked treats increased as he moved toward it. He sat down at an outside table and from there James could see the store the man had entered: a barbershop.

He ordered coffee, not caring whether it arrived before his potentially sudden departure. He drew his cell again, fully intending to use it this time.

"Samuel," James said, "I just ran into an old friend, Kevin Atkinson."

"Pulling the files now," Samuel responded. Samuel was having a very busy day. "Was this a mutual meeting?"

"Negative thus far," James replied. "But, I'm sure he'll let me know soon if he's planning to catch up with me."

"I'm sure he will, old friends are good like that. Sending you the files now."

"Thanks, I'll be in touch," James said, ending the call. He would read the files soon, but for now his attention was on that store, and the man whom he was waiting to exit.

It looked to be a small barbershop, the traditional kind that usually had one or two older men working. Everything about the situation pointed to a random coincidence, but that wasn't enough for James. Their meeting might've been coincidental, but when destiny aligned there was usually a good reason for it. Sometimes it was revealed immediately, sometimes months later, or even years later. But destiny always had a plan.

It was strange to see someone from his past, and James felt a pull within him. There was a slice of his soul that missed his life in the agency. If it hadn't been so corrupt, he probably never would have left. And he certainly would not have left in the way he had. Groups like the CIA are needed, and their work is important, but the problem with power is, for most people, the more they get the more they want. They become greedy, and greedy hands can quickly become dirty.

When James had crossed over to the CIA he had been given the opportunity of his career—the opportunity of a lifetime—or so he had thought. His role had been to head up a new division of intelligence—a division with no boundaries and no rules. A division that had not been, and never would be, officially acknowledged. James and his team had been the ghosts of the CIA with one purpose: gather intelligence on Russia's bioweapon program—bioweapons with the potential to inflict horrors unknown to mankind. The memo had been to steal the information and give it to the CIA so vaccines could be created, spelling the end of Russia's power over the world. In theory it had been a good plan, but that wasn't how things had turned out.

James had taken a mere two sips from his coffee when his old friend exited the barbershop. He carried himself in a way that James recognized—casual but careful. He surveyed the street, but he didn't seem to be looking for James—he was looking for a shadow behind him that shouldn't be there. James watched him astutely, monitoring his body language. He presented no obvious threat to James so he simply watched his silhouette shrink with each step until he disappeared completely. James was never one to go looking for a situation, but if one presented itself, you could be sure he wouldn't walk away from it.

James paid his bill and then walked back to where his car was parked. He drove back to his apartment and only then, when he was certain he was safe, did he open Kevin's files.

James sat down at the dining table and opened his laptop. He scrolled through the pages of electronic documents, more concerned with what Kevin had been up to in recent years. He was supposedly retired, but that could mean anything in the CIA world, with his last location identified as Lebanon six years ago. There was nothing recent in his file, which meant Kevin had kept a very low profile—or it had been deleted. James saw nothing of interest, but he mentally filed the meeting away as an incident not to be forgotten.

He logged into the Thomas Security database and pulled up the surveillance Samuel had running on Roberts. Since his meeting with the Docoss Hotel manager early that morning, monitoring him had become a little easier due to the recording chip James had installed under his shirt collar. It had been easy to place without him realizing, because with a pistol pointed at your temple you were less alert to what else was going on.

Samuel's team would alert him if Roberts did anything suspect, but James wanted to watch the man himself. He was sitting at his computer, working, but his body language told James he was on edge. His shoulders were sitting higher to his ears—tight with tension—and his eyes kept flickering from his computer to the door of his office like he might be expecting someone. James minimized the footage window and moved it to the top corner of his screen while he opened Mak's file. He was interested to see the photographs of the ring. James loaded them, and then enlarged and refocused them. The ring looked tarnished, and there appeared to be no biological fluid stains. It looked old, and it looked dirty. James checked for indents, or any major scratches that might indicate it had been forcibly removed, but he couldn't identify any. Early forensic results would be back within a few hours, James calculated, but until then he would have to wait.

People often assumed James's life was one action-adventure after another, but a large portion of it was a waiting game. Waiting for information that could change people's lives forever.

6

MAK ASHWOOD

Maya sat across from Mak, devouring a chocolate croissant. Mak had no appetite, her mind distracted by thoughts of Eric's ring and how her mother had come to find it.

"I think you're making too much of this," Maya said. "It's weird, for sure, but you know what Mom is like—she's always moving things around that house. I think Eric took it off last time he was there, and Mom had moved something, probably one of those awful doily things she so loves, and it fell on the floor."

Mak wanted to accept such an explanation, but it seemed too strange after all of these years.

Mak's cell phone rang, and she picked it up immediately.

"Hey," Mak said, keeping her voice neutral. She hadn't told Maya what was going on with James yet; it seemed pointless until she had made up her mind.

"Hey, Mak," James said. "I've just looked over the initial forensics reports for Eric's ring. They will do further testing over the next few days, but at this stage the ring appropriately reflects that it has been sitting somewhere dusty, untouched for many years. Nothing indicates it was forcibly removed, nor are there any bloodstains or unexpected DNA on the ring. Forensics are going to process specialized

DNA testing, but given the time period, and the fact that any DNA potentially on the ring at the time Eric disappeared hasn't been preserved, we're not expecting to find any other sources. But, we'll check anyway."

She'd gotten herself all worked up for nothing. And why? What did she expect to come of finding the ring?

"Thanks, James. I appreciate it," Mak said.

"Sure. Is Maya there?"

"Yes," Mak said.

"Good. I'll let you go."

"Thanks, again." Mak put her cell phone down on the table and raised her eyes to meet Maya's.

"Nothing," Mak said, shrugging her shoulders. "The ring looks like it's been sitting somewhere untouched all these years. He must've taken it off the last time we were there. I should've noticed he wasn't wearing his ring."

Maya's eyes flickered to the left corner of the room, which they always did when she was thinking something through. "You were right in the middle of exams, correct? Maybe you were just preoccupied?"

Mak sighed, leaning forward to survey the range of pastries Maya brought with her. Mak's appetite had returned.

"I was. Right in the thick of it. Still, I think that's something I should've noticed," Mak said, sliding the blueberry tart halfway out of its paper sleeve. She took a small bite. "Damn, this is good," Mak said, taking a second, much larger bite.

Maya chuckled. "They're from a new bakery that opened around the corner from our apartment. There is a line out the door every morning."

Maya finished off her own pastry and let out a contented sigh. She scrunched the paper bag up into a ball and pushed it into the center of the table.

"So, now that the ring saga is resolved, let's talk about more exciting things. I've found this beautiful, quaint villa for us to stay in for the first few nights in Spain. Is there anything you want to see in particular? Or should we just book things as we go? I think that's best, because then we have a lot more flexibility with the itinerary. You have a few weeks off, right?"

Maya's rambling about Spain made Mak's chest tighten. If she said yes to James, she couldn't go—at least not without him.

"Perhaps, but don't book anything yet, Maya," Mak said casually.

"What? Why not?" Maya pulled a face indicating she didn't like the direction of this conversation.

"Because, Thomas Security is still worried about the potential fallout of me winning that trial," Mak said. "I'm currently still on high alert, which is why you're here today, remember. I don't know how long until this is resolved."

Maya leaned forward, crossing her elbows on the table. Her lips wiggled side to side. "It's still a few months away, surely it will be fine. If not, can't you just take Cami with you?"

Ordinarily, that might suffice if her risk was downgraded. But the real excuse for not being able to go was James Thomas. And it annoyed Mak that she had to think about compromising in this issue. "I don't know, Maya. I don't know what is going on or what these brothers are thinking the majority of the time." *And that isn't a lie.*

Maya looked like she suddenly remembered where they were. She wet her lips. "Can we investigate this place?"

A small laugh slipped through Mak's lips. "What did you have in mind? Every door seems to have an access code—which conveniently hasn't been given to me—and I've been able to ascertain very little of what is on each floor."

That only seemed to make Maya more excited. "Come on, let's just walk around and see what we can find." She looked around the room. "It beats the alternative, right?"

Mak felt like they were children again, playing games similar to the ones they used to play in their grandparents' house. They stood, leaving the remaining pastries on the table. Mak didn't think they'd get far and the pastries would still be warm when they returned. Or were returned. Mak slipped her cell phone into her back pocket and followed Maya to the door.

Maya opened it and stuck her head out into the hallway, like a spy in a movie.

"You're an idiot," Mak said, laughing.

"Left or right?" Maya said with a giggle.

Mak didn't want to go left or right. She wanted to go to the basement, to B2. But she didn't want to go to the shooting range like she had yesterday; she wanted to see what was at the other end of that hallway. There was something about the way Cami had said 'Secrets' that had intrigued Mak.

"Go to the elevators," Mak said. "Quickly."

Mak wondered if they were being watched, but she knew one thing for sure—the faster they moved the better. Inside the elevator, Mak swiped the security pass she had been given and pressed B2. She had half expected it not to activate but the button lit up red and they moved.

"Where are we going?" Maya whispered.

"To the place of secrets," Mak responded, watching her sister's face transform with delight.

"What do you mean? What is in the basement?"

"I honestly don't know, and I don't think I'm supposed to. So, of course, that makes me more curious," Mak said.

Maya's eyes lifted to the display panel as the numbers descended with each floor. When they arrived at B2, Mak led Maya into the empty hallway, which was as quiet as a deserted city. There was no one to be seen, not a voice to be heard. They were all alone—it seemed.

"See," Mak said, nodding her head toward a door they passed. "Every room has a lock and code."

"Hmm."

They walked quietly, almost tiptoeing through the empty hallway, until Mak stopped at the last set of double doors.

"Now what?" Maya whispered, putting her ear to the door. She shook her head, which Mak thought was an indication she couldn't hear anything. They definitely needed to work on their non-verbal spy communication.

"If we enter an incorrect code, what do you think will happen?"

Mak didn't get a chance to find out because the door suddenly swung open and Maya jumped back, screaming in shock.

A man stood before them with an amused grin on his face. "You ladies seem to be lost."

Mak peered around him, trying to get a look behind the doors but he shifted in line with her vision, blocking her.

He took a step forward and closed the door behind him. "I can't show you this room, but I'm going to take you somewhere much more fun, believe me."

Mak and Maya looked at each other, and then followed him back toward the elevator. Mak could imagine Cami sitting somewhere, watching them, clutching her chest as she laughed.

The man held the stairwell door open for them like a gentleman. "One floor up," he said.

They exited the stairwell, and he entered a code into the door directly across the hallway. When it opened, Mak knew what it was: the game room.

And in true Thomas Security fashion, it was spectacular. Mak's eyes traveled over the pool table, the arcade machines, the foosball table, and at last settled on the Ping-Pong table. Mak and Maya's eyes met: it was game time.

"Well, this wasn't quite the intended destination," Mak said, looking at her sister, "but while we're here we may as well play."

The man who had escorted them from the basement spoke again. "Everything you'll need, for any of these games, you can find in these cupboards." He held out his hand to a wall of cabinets, and Mak made her way over to them.

She opened one and saw everything was labeled and neatly organized. Her search moved to the next cupboard, and there she found some paddles and balls.

Maya came up behind her, looking over her shoulder. "Someone has an obsessive tendency. Actually, every inch of this building that I've seen is immaculate. How many staff do they have?"

She hadn't witnessed a lot of staff, but James had told her a maid would clean up the theater room after them. James himself, though, seemed to be very tidy. She wondered if that was indicative of his past —men with military backgrounds were usually very organized and routine based. Not that she could confirm he had been in the military, but he'd definitely been in a line of work that had allowed him to acquire some very interesting skills.

"I have no idea," Mak said, closing the cupboard door.

Maya took a paddle and moved toward the table, circling her arms like she were warming up. Mak laughed—competitiveness was rife in their family.

"It's been a long time since I've played," Maya said. "And, therefore, I think it's only fair we have a few games to dust off the old limbs. What do you say?"

"Sure," Mak said as she bounced the ball onto the table and powered a shot directly at Maya.

"Mak!" her sister scolded, unprepared for the attack.

Mak chuckled. "Sorry, I couldn't help myself—it was too good an opportunity to miss." Mak suddenly wished James was at the other end. Although if he had been, he probably would've fired that shot right back at her. Mak got the feeling that James wasn't the kind of person who would let her win.

"Two can play that game, Makkie," Maya said, arrogantly.

The warm-up round was a good indication of how their games would progress. There was a lot of risk-taking, a lot of cheating, and a lot of verbal slinging designed to distract.

In fact, Mak was so engrossed in the game she barely realized when Deacon Thomas walked in.

7

JAMES THOMAS

"Where were they going?" James asked Samuel, who was filling him in on Mak and Maya's adventures.

"Apparently, they wanted to take themselves on a tour of our morgue," Samuel said.

A chuckle slipped through James's lips. *That would've been an interesting conversation.*

"Fred just happened to be in there doing some maintenance on the refrigerators," Samuel said, "so I told him to go and open the door. It scared the living daylights out of them. You should've seen Maya scream." Samuel was laughing to himself, and James knew Mak Ashwood had provided him with more entertainment in recent weeks than Samuel had had in years.

"Keep a close eye on her, Samuel," James warned, but it was a lighthearted statement—there was little Mak would be able to see without their access codes, no matter how many corridors she walked. "What are they doing now?" James asked.

"There is quite an aggressive Ping-Pong tournament going on. And Deacon, of course, is only fueling the situation. He's even called in Tom so they can play doubles," Samuel said.

James felt a pinch of envy in his chest: he wanted to be there, he wanted to be the one playing against her. But this was the reality of his life—it wasn't fun; it never had been, and it was unlikely it ever would be. It wasn't a bad life, in fact James had come to love it, but he would never get to experience the carefree lives others lived.

"At least she's entertained," James said and Samuel agreed, although James wondered if Samuel had heard the disappointment in his words. "Where are we at with that ring?" James continued. There was no point dwelling on what could be—he had two major security situations to resolve, and both were moving achingly slow.

"It's going to be a few more hours until we get the specialized forensics back, although I doubt they will tell us much. I am, however, looking at something a little strange. The CCTV footage I've been reviewing . . . it looks like someone has been doing some editing work. Someone very good."

James' heart sank. "Continue."

"I don't know what it means yet, but I think someone deleted a portion of the film and duplicated another portion, making up the time difference. I've also been looking at the photographs of the kitchen buffet. I really don't think it could have fallen off something. The overhead cabinets have doors, and there aren't any ledges, or anything similar, that it could've been sitting on unnoticed. My guess, now that I've seen this issue with the CCTV footage, is that it was placed there. I think someone entered their home, which has basically no security other than a simple alarm, and placed the ring."

James turned it over in his mind, chewing on his bottom lip as he thought it through. "I really don't like this," James said. "We need to make sure we're keeping an open mind to every possible option."

Samuel sighed. "Agreed. What message are they trying to send, though?"

"I don't know." And he truly had no idea. If this had happened a year or two after Eric had gone missing, James would've thought it was a message for Mak. A message for her not to give up, not to believe he was dead. But after this long? James had to assume it was something more sinister, that someone was playing games with her—mind games.

"What are you going to be able to find out about this CCTV footage? Can you link back the hack to a server or location?" James asked.

"It's a very clean hack, which if they are capable of doing that means they're probably not stupid enough to disclose any details in the process," Samuel said.

They were a step behind, and James hated to be in that position. A security team was now stationed at Mak's parents' house, but James seriously doubted there was any risk to them. They had left the ring and given her a message. The task now was to decipher the message.

James had one long-term plan up his sleeve that could generate new leads—something he knew would cause a reaction—but it was far too early to use it. But if this situation escalated, there was one way they could change the game, and that would be for Samuel to move Eric's money. Then things would get really interesting.

"Keep me updated. I'm going to have a look through these CIA files related to the reservation list attendee, Troy Taylor," James said, looking down at his laptop. "I'm also simultaneously watching Mr. Roberts, but so far so good on that situation."

"Agreed. I'll touch base again as soon as the full forensics come through," Samuel said and hung up.

James focused his attention on profiling Troy Taylor. Like most of the CIA files, his early years were noticeably absent, but they certainly had been taking detailed notes over the past ten years. He'd been out of the agency about as long as James had, but he'd left for other reasons—not to wreak revenge on the corrupt souls of the agency, but to further his own greedy hands. Troy Taylor had been living in Iraq, collecting intelligence on its nuclear weapons program. At some point, however, he'd entangled himself so completely he seemed to have lost sense of right and wrong, and had apparently stolen prototypes and then disappeared. What he'd been doing since was either not known or not reported. The CIA came close to finding him on a few occasions, but he'd managed to slip through its web. So he was good, and he was going to be difficult to capture alive. James would need an extra set of hands, Deacon's hands. So what to do with Mak?

It was a question he had weeks to answer. And life could completely change in two weeks—as he knew all too well.

He looked at his bag on the floor, ready to go at a moment's notice. This was his life, and the gravity of it sat heavier than it ever had. In the past months he'd changed in ways he'd never thought possible, and the more time that passed since the events in Paris, the more he understood just how much effect they'd had on him. He'd been naïve to think those events wouldn't change him.

Paris had been the biggest mistake of his life. And one he couldn't fix.

James hadn't been lying when he'd told Mak he didn't do relationships, because he didn't. He had, however, had one casual relationship that had changed everything. He'd known Angela for over ten years. They had worked together in the CIA, and the attraction had always been there and had always been mutual. It was convenient for both of them because they understood each other's backgrounds, and she understood his need for it to be nothing more than sex. James had thought it was the perfect arrangement—how wrong he'd been.

James trusted so few people, and as a result, he watched everyone around him—including her. Samuel found out she was informing on him and feeding information back to the CIA. She'd tell them when he was visiting and how long he was staying. Samuel had found this out two days before her fateful telephone call—the one saying she needed to talk to him urgently. James arrived a day earlier than expected, and he hadn't been interested in hearing her excuses or her lies, so when he'd let himself into her home, he greeted her with three bullets in her chest—that was how he dealt with people who betrayed him.

She'd had no warning, and no indication he was there. Her body fell to the floor, and he'd stepped over it as he walked to her office. He took his time ransacking her belongings, looking for anything about him, or any other useful intelligence, when he stumbled across something he'd never expected to find. An ultrasound. His eyes darted to the date: it had been taken one week before. His legs had gone numb as he'd looked over his shoulder at her still body in the hallway. He'd looked at her stomach, the oversized sweater now lying flat against her body, and saw a slight swelling of her waist. He'd run toward her, then found himself kneeling over her lifeless body. He'd checked her breathing and her pulse, but she had neither—he'd always been a good shot.

Panic had consumed him as he'd tried to resuscitate her, fruitlessly, until Samuel—who had been watching the events unfold and listening in via his earpiece—said softly: "Stop, James, stop. It's done."

James remembered sitting in her hallway, slumped over her body, for what seemed like hours. Samuel later confirmed he had been there four hours. At last, when his senses returned, he knew he had to confirm—one hundred percent—that the baby was his. He ran to the nearest hospital and helped himself to their supplies, taking two large biopsy needles and returned to Angela's apartment. His fingers had trembled as he'd stabbed the first needle into her womb, hoping to get enough fluid to be able to do a DNA test. He'd stuck a second needle in as a backup. He transferred the samples to the tubes and then, with the help of Samuel, tracked down a local laboratory that would analyze them for him—a gun to the head was a powerful motivator.

While he waited for the results he tormented himself with questions. How had this happened? He'd always used protection, except on one occasion when he didn't have any, so he'd pulled out early. A risk he'd taken only because she'd had an intrauterine device. But as Samuel busily pieced together her recent movements, they'd found out she'd secretly had the IUD removed. It was almost impossible the child was his, but it was a possibility. But why would she have had the device removed? Was it a safeguard so if he ever found out she had informed on him he wouldn't kill her? It was the only explanation he'd been able to come up with, but he'd never know for sure.

The results came back conclusive.

He had murdered his unborn son.

8

MAK ASHWOOD

Mak combed through her long, platinum blond locks and secured them at the base of her head in a low ponytail. She looked at herself in the mirror, decided she needed a touch more blush on her cheeks, and then she was ready—ready to face the legal world again. A weekend spent in Thomas Security seemed so removed from the real world that it had been easy to forget about the trial verdict and the security threats. She'd been entertained and distracted all weekend—which had been good, but she deemed it no accident.

Deacon Thomas was no replacement for James, but he'd been a good companion yesterday. And he was a good competitor. They'd won the doubles contest in Ping-Pong, much to Maya's dismay, and then he'd organized dinner for them all, which they'd eaten on the rooftop.

James hadn't been joking when he'd said they like to leave as little as possible, and Mak now saw this building for what it was: it wasn't just a home, it was a fortress. And if you needed to live in a palace of security such as this, you had made enemies, and a lot of them. James had already told her as much; he'd told her he had punished the men who had misled him, but only now was the severity of his words setting in.

"Mak?" Cami's voice sounded through the apartment.

"I'm ready," Mak called out, turning off the bathroom light. She quickly checked her phone, but there was nothing from James. Mak hadn't spoken to him since he'd called back with the initial forensics news, and she wondered when she would hear from him again. She didn't want to call him because she had no idea what he was doing, and she didn't want to disrupt him while he was in the middle of something important.

When Mak walked into the lounge she was surprised to see Deacon with Cami. She raised one eyebrow and he smiled.

"We need to be very careful today," he said. The tone of his voice was casual, in contrast to the meaning of his words.

"Right," Mak said as she followed them out and to the car. There were three cars waiting with their engines purring when they arrived. Mak couldn't see through the tinted windows, but she had a good suspicion that every car was full of bodyguards, except for the three seats they needed.

Deacon opened the door for her, and slid in next to her. Cami sat on her other side.

"This is cozy," Mak remarked and Cami chuckled. Deacon gave a little smile.

Mak looked to the driver's seat, which was usually occupied by Deacon, but she didn't recognize the man there now.

"You can relax," Deacon said. "It's our job to worry about the security and make sure you're safe, you just need to go about your normal day."

"Easier said than done," Mak responded.

"So, what is on your agenda today, now that the trial has finished?" Cami asked.

"A lot of paperwork, I imagine. I also received an email over the weekend from my boss about another case he was looking at last week. I don't have a lot of details yet, but I saw that my assistant scheduled a meeting about it this afternoon, so I'll find out soon enough."

"Have private legal firms contacted you in the past?" Deacon asked. "Head hunted, as such? I imagine there might be some offers coming your way after the success of the last trial."

"They have," Mak said. "I'm not interested in working in the private sector, though."

"Even if the offer was incredible?" Deacon asked.

Mak refolded the cuff of her shirt so it sat properly. "Well, never say never, I suppose. But I can't imagine an offer that would be good enough to convince me."

"Fair enough," Deacon said, his gaze diverting to the traffic ahead. Mak watched his eyes as they carefully roamed the streets and passing cars. Like his brother, Deacon Thomas was always very attentive to their surroundings.

They pulled up at the front of Mak's office building and, as per protocol, she was instructed to stay in the car until the security team had assembled themselves. Mak could see media on the footpath—media she didn't want to deal with. She had nothing new to say today; her thoughts had not changed since Friday. She still wanted to retry Kate's case, but she wouldn't push the family to do it.

"Do you want to go straight inside or talk to the media?" Cami asked.

"Straight in," Mak said without hesitation.

Deacon opened the door and took her hand, helping her out of the car. She was immediately escorted in, and when they were safely inside the building, both Deacon and Cami stayed by her side. Deacon took a post outside her office, while Cami sat in her office with her.

It was slightly distracting, but soon enough Mak was absorbed with the flurry of her workload and she soon forgot about Cami. Thomas Security was skilled at that—their presence was everywhere, but they were easy to forget. Excluding James Thomas.

The shrill tone of Mak's office phone pulled her from her thoughts.

"Mak Ashwood."

"Hey, Mak. It's Kayla. How are you?"

Mak smiled and relaxed back into her chair. She felt so removed from her social life that it was nice to hear Kayla's voice again. "I'm good. How is the case going?"

"Ugh, it's killing me. Sometimes I wonder why I went into the medico-legal field, and other days I love it. The case should be wrapping up in a few weeks, though. How are things?"

"Much the same," Mak said vaguely, trying to follow the Thomas brothers' instructions not to talk about her security situation.

"How are things with James?"

Mak paused, more aware than usual of her current lack of privacy. No longer could she have a casual conversation about a guy she was interested in without being listened in on.

"Much the same there, too," Mak said.

"I see . . ." Kayla said and Mak knew she didn't have to tell her the conversation was being monitored—Kayla wasn't an idiot. "Well," Kayla continued, "I just wanted to let you know my parents are coming to Manhattan for the weekend and are taking me out to dinner as an early birthday present. I'd love you to come, but I know it might be a bit difficult given the current situation."

Kayla's relationship with her family was still strained after her drug-addict past, but slowly she was repairing the damage she'd done. She'd recently been welcomed into her parents' home for the first time in nearly fifteen years, and Mak knew how much this dinner must mean to her friend.

"Kayla, that's wonderful. That's a big step forward," Mak said.

"It is," Kayla agreed. "I never thought I could fix things with my family, but I guess with forgiveness anything is possible." Kayla sighed. "I've made some really bad decisions in my past, Mak, things I wish with all my heart I could undo."

Mak didn't know what her friend was alluding to, but Mak knew spending several years addicted to cocaine would lead to some less than impressive decisions.

"Maybe not," Mak said, not wanting to offer a false assurance to her friend. "But you're making good decisions now, and that's what is important."

"I hope so. Anyway," Kayla said, "do you think there is even a slight chance you might be able to come to dinner?"

"I'll ask, but I highly doubt it," Mak said regretfully.

When she hung up the phone she did ask, and the answer was a resounding "no."

Late that afternoon, Mak attended the scheduled meeting with her boss, Mr. Bill Mead. They had a good relationship, and Mak had a lot of respect for the district attorney. Someday she wanted his job, but now she was content to learn from him. One day she might even be better than he was.

Cami escorted Mak to Bill's office, but this was one meeting she didn't attend, although she did sit right outside.

"I'm impressed by this security firm," Bill said. "But from what I've been observing, and the level of protection they're providing, I'm not sure you've been totally honest about the security threats you've received." Bill folded his large hands over his waist as he settled back into his chair behind his desk.

Mak sat down in the chair opposite him. "I personally think they're a bit extreme, even they say they are, but they don't like to take risks—so what you see is the result of that."

Bill looked at her with a half-grin. "You didn't answer the question, Mak."

"I received a few notes, the notes you heard about in the media. And one night the car taking me home was involved in a little bit of a collision. Since then, there have been no incidents, and I'm confident there won't be."

It was a white lie—Mak wasn't confident there wouldn't be any more incidents, but she was confident that Thomas Security could deal with them.

Bill stared her down, and Mak felt like she was a witness on the stand. "Be careful, Mak. It was a big case, with lots of media attention. There could be fallout from that—I should know."

Bill did know. He'd been shot once, during a case, but had thankfully lived to see many more days.

"Believe me," Mak said, "I can barely breathe without being monitored at the moment. I'm going to be fine."

Bill gave an unconvinced sigh, but leaned forward and slid a manila folder toward her. He was a good boss because he cared about his staff, but he also knew when to get on with the job.

"As you know, this came my way last week. I've been looking over it, waiting for your trial to finish before I formally brought it your way. It's interesting, and it's a very difficult case, but I think you'll enjoy it."

Mak opened the manila folder, her eyes scanning over its contents. The victim was a Tribecca man, shot dead in his home six years ago. One man had been tried and convicted, but his case had been reopened due to new evidence.

"What are your initial thoughts?" Mak asked with downcast eyes —she was looking over the evidence photographs.

"The evidence is circumstantial, and there is a doubt in my mind that the right man was convicted. We could have an innocent man in prison, and a killer on the loose."

Mak took in a tight breath between her teeth that sounded almost like a whistle. "The original prosecutor . . ." Mak said, looking through the documents for the name.

"He's unfortunately passed on—dropped dead of a major heart attack about a year after this case."

"Oh," Mak said.

"Take the files, look it over, think about it, and we'll catch up again tomorrow," Bill said.

Mak stood up, holding the file in her hand, and when she went to leave, Bill spoke up again. "By the way, great job, Mak. You nailed it."

Mak put on her fake smile and thanked him.

He gave a sarcastic laugh. "You're too much like me," he muttered as he looked down at the papers on his desk.

Mak closed the door behind her and, with Cami back at her side, went to the kitchen to make coffee and then back to her office to review the case. She would need to get her assistant to download all of the electronic files onto her computer, and retrieve any paper files. And so it began again, another case to lose herself in.

As the evening drew near, Mak decided to stay at work late and continue looking over the case. They ordered in food, and when Deacon Thomas walked in Mak thought he was delivering dinner, but instead he sat down in the chair opposite her desk.

"Interesting case?" he asked, nodding at the chaos of folders on her desk.

"Honestly, I'm not sure what to make of it as yet," Mak said, trying to guess the reason for his visit.

He lifted his hips enough to pull out what looked to be a small zip-lock bag. Only when he handed it to her did Mak realize what was inside: Eric's ring.

She took it hesitantly and stared at it for the moment, until she noticed Deacon watching her carefully.

"Forensics have done all of the tests that they can, so I figured we should return it to you," he said.

Mak nodded her head, but she felt unsure what to do with it. "What are your thoughts on how this ring was found?"

James had told her there was nothing suspect about the ring itself, but last night, while lying in bed and giving it thought, she'd realized he hadn't revealed how he'd thought it came to be under her mother's buffet.

Deacon gave a slight shrug of his shoulders. "It had to have fallen out of something your mother, or perhaps even your father, moved. We can't conclude anything else, can we?"

Mak opened the plastic bag and took out the ring. It had all the little signs of everyday wear that was to be expected. She read over the inscription again: *Forever and Always*. How wrong they had been.

Mak put the ring back in the bag and put it in her desk drawer, next to her own ring—a sight she'd never thought she'd see.

"Thanks," Mak said as casually as she could, but truth be told, the ring incited a sense of guilt—she should've paid more attention to her husband. How could she not have noticed he wasn't wearing his wedding ring? Had he told her he'd left it at her parents' house, and she'd simply forgotten? If he had, Mak thought she would've at least asked her mom to put the ring somewhere safe, but she hadn't mentioned anything either. It was strange, but his entire disappearance was strange.

"How long are you planning to stay at the office tonight?" Deacon asked.

Mak flicked her wrist, checking the time. "Another few hours, if that's okay?"

"Of course it is, it doesn't matter to us, but if we have a vague idea of your schedule it helps coordinate the team," he said, standing to leave.

"Sure," Mak said, watching Deacon as he walked past Cami. Mak saw Cami raise her eyes to meet his, hold his gaze, and then blink once before diverting her gaze back to the hallway she had been watching for hours.

Was that some form of non-verbal communication? Was something going on she should know about? Mak continued to watch Cami but she did nothing further that piqued Mak's intrigue.

Mak thought about it for a moment, wondering if she was overanalyzing, but something instinctively told her she'd witnessed something she wasn't supposed to.

Was it about the ring?

9

JAMES THOMAS

"I'm watching," James said, his eyes transfixed on the surveillance screens monitoring Mak's office building.

Deacon was in the lobby, taking a proactive position to the situation but James's foot tapped on the floor regardless. It was hard to sit in an apartment on another continent and watch as a former Special Forces soldier stalked Mak's office. When James was on site, in the midst of the scenario, his intuition and years of training guided him. But sitting back, watching events unfold with very little control other than issuing verbal commands, which could be delayed due to the geographical distances, was hard. Especially when the person they were protecting was Mak Ashwood.

Samuel had identified the soldier via their facial recognition software. It was the guy who had gotten away the night Mak's car was rammed and James had taken her to the Tivoli Hotel. James watched as he walked in the direction of her building. They'd first identified him four blocks away on a seemingly late-night stroll. The man had stopped for a pack of cigarettes and subsequently lit one up and casually enjoyed it. Nothing about him seemed suspect—but everything about him was.

When did the mafia start recruiting, or contracting, Special Forces guys?

It was a piece of the puzzle that didn't fit, and it continued to trouble James.

The soldier stopped again and lit another cigarette. He was either a chain-smoker, or he was using it as a prop—James thought the latter. Special Forces soldiers, even ex-soldiers, weren't generally smokers because they knew what the toxic gas did to their fitness. They might have an occasional one, but it was rare for them to smoke at the rate of this soldier.

"Circle back," Deacon instructed to a second team that was moving in from the south. They were attempting to cast a net, one that would hopefully capture the soldier.

"I want him alive," James said, reminding his team not to get too gun-happy.

If the soldier was alive, he was capable of talking, and there was never a man James hadn't been able to get to talk. Albeit, sadly, he wouldn't be doing this potential interrogation—Deacon would have the honor—but James had trained Deacon to be as barbaric as he was. Deacon didn't get the same thrill from it that James did, but he got the same results. And that was all that mattered.

"Samuel," James said, "I want to see his face, as close as you can."

"Copy," Samuel said, and the camera zoomed in and re-focused. It wasn't a great picture, but it was enough.

James could see the man's eyes darting from side to side and up and down. He was watching, watching very carefully.

The soldier had either seriously underestimated Mak's security, or he was a bold man willing to take a few risks to get close to her.

It is possible he's underestimated her security. The evening Mak's car had been involved in the collision, they'd set off flashbangs. Flashbangs were a brilliant device, in that they caused no harm to those around them, but if you weren't expecting one to go off, they effectively dazzled you. It made it very difficult to see properly and to keep track of everyone's movements. From a defense position, they were gold, from an attacker's position, they were a nightmare.

And how would the soldier know anything about Thomas Security and how good they were? James wasn't biased; their reputation was built on success, and the reason for it was the four key players in the company had backgrounds and training that were unparalleled. They weren't bodyguards who had progressed up the ranks and then decided to start a company. They had all been the elite of their fields, joined together as one force, and it was a recipe for success. And as far as James knew, there was currently no firm that matched them. Not even internationally—that's why clients paid millions of dollars per year for their services. It would be easy to underestimate them, and that might be this soldier's biggest mistake.

"I'm not getting any verbal communication or static traces from him," Samuel said. *"I think he's alone."*

James looked at the yellow dots on the screen. They were his men, slowly, carefully, inching through the streets of Manhattan, tightening the web around this man. The situation was looking in their favor, but James knew that could change at any moment.

The soldier stubbed out his cigarette, pulled a phone from his back pocket, and held it to his ear.

"Feeding audio," Samuel said.

"Hi . . . I'm doing well . . . Quiet night . . . No . . . I'll find out soon . . . Bye."

James replayed the conversation in his head, wishing he'd been able to hear the other half of the conversation. It was too short of a call to get a trace, especially with no other intelligence to help Samuel.

I'll find out soon.

The man started walking again, his eyes flickering to the rooftops. *He's checking for snipers.*

"Close in. Tom, move sixty feet west," Deacon instructed, and James watched as the yellow circles came closer together.

They still needed to wait, but Deacon knew not to wait until this man was at Mak's building. They wouldn't let him get that close—they were going to make a move before then, and if the team could do it without Deacon, all the better.

James didn't want his brother risked because he needed him healthy and ready for the interrogation. And, preferably, in Mak's building the entire time this went down. It was a good thing she'd wanted to stay for a few more hours because it meant they didn't have to keep her in the building unwillingly, and therefore reveal any details of the situation. The less she knew the better—it was the same for all of their clients.

"Hold," Deacon said.

James sat up, leaning closer to the two laptops he had set on the dining table. The soldier had taken an unexpected turn down a passageway two blocks from Mak's building. James didn't want his team scrambling, not when it could be a decoy.

What are you doing? James mentally placed himself in the man's shoes, trying to predict his next move.

He was out of view in the passageway, which, if he was trying to avoid surveillance, was a good move. The problem with passageways, though, was there were few exits.

And the additional problem for the solider was Thomas Security's men had night vision with thermal-imaging technology strapped to their eyes.

"Jack, move in, hold at the corner," Deacon said.

It was closer than James wanted one of his men to be, but like his brother, he also didn't want this guy to move off surveillance. It was their chance to get answers, and they couldn't let him slip away again.

"Copy."

A few seconds later James could see the soldier again—via Jack's glasses that fed through to Samuel—but he was no longer on the ground; he was climbing up the building wall like Spiderman.

"Jack, fire one shot to the leg," Deacon said.

And don't fucking miss.

Jack didn't miss. And chaos erupted.

The soldier pulled a pistol and fired back as he fell to the ground.

"Move in!" Deacon said, and the yellow dots sped toward one another, joining together like fluorescent clusters of mold.

The soldier fired round after round as he attempted to rescale the wall, but another shot hit his leg and his body fell to ground; his head rebounded as it did.

"*Target captured,*" Jack said as he stood at the soldier's limp body. "*Target unresponsive . . . Pulse identified.*"

"*Well done, team. Move out now,*" Deacon said, audibly exhaling.

They had the soldier, and provided he didn't have brain damage from that fall, when he finally came to he would realize he'd woken up in hell.

James rubbed his neck, watching as his men loaded the soldier into a van and escorted him back to Thomas Security. He watched the van and accompanying cars for the entire journey. Only when they were safely inside, sans ambush, with the soldier secured in a cell, did James concede the mission a success.

James changed the security surveillance windows to show the footage of Mak's office. She seemed lost in thought, absorbed in her work, and James felt a pang of relief. She was safe—for now.

It was another hour before Mak was ready to leave, and James passed the time by drinking coffee and monitoring the surveillance screens. The soldier had come around, and he'd squeezed his eyes shut when he'd realized he was being held captive. He didn't know where he was, or who they were, or what was destined for him—but he was smart enough to know it wasn't good.

James watched as Mak was escorted home, and Cami took her up to her apartment. Deacon bid them goodnight, but he didn't go straight to the cells.

"What are you doing?" James asked, watching his brother keenly.

"*Fueling up,*" Deacon said as he opened the door to Samuel's office.

James thought he ate a lot, but nothing compared to Deacon's appetite. And there was almost always food in Samuel's office, because it was the meeting point after their very long days.

"*How is our guest doing?*" Deacon asked Samuel.

"*He's awake, which is good news, but he's going to be a hard one to crack, I think. He's looking around the cell like he thinks there must be some way he can get out of it. He's not going to talk easily,"* Samuel said.

"All the more fun then, right, James?" Deacon said.

"Exactly, brother," James said and Samuel scoffed.

Deacon took his time eating, although it wasn't a bad thing—it gave their soldier more time to think. And to worry. And to get anxious. But when Deacon finally walked into the cells, James was on the edge of his seat—this was his favorite kind of movie to watch.

10

JAMES THOMAS

Deacon stood at the threshold of the cell, leaning against the metal bars with his arms crossed over his chest. The soldier lifted his eyes to meet Deacon's, his brows knitting together as his eyes slimmed into a squint.

"Who are you?" the soldier asked.

Deacon waited a few seconds before answering, drawing out the anticipation. *"That is none of your concern,"* he said, taking two slow steps toward the man bound to the chair. *"What is your concern, however, is talking. You're going to be doing a lot of it, and I'm sure you know there are two ways we can go about this. You can offer up the information you have, or I can force it out of you. If I were you, I would take the first option."*

The soldier jutted his jaw forward in seeming resistance.

Deacon drew a pair of pliers from his back pocket—there was another reason the brothers' uniforms included jeans—their favorite brand had lots of useful pockets.

James saw the soldier's eyes dilate—the man knew Deacon wasn't bluffing, and he fully realized his fate. Deacon stood directly in front of the soldier now, and the cameras surveying the cell adjusted appropriately—thanks to Samuel. Deacon tapped the pliers against the palm of his left hand, his eyes never leaving the soldier.

"Who are you working for?" Deacon asked.

The man's face stonewalled—he was not going to talk voluntarily.

"Last chance," Deacon warned.

The man's chest expanded as he inhaled deeply, but his lips remained closed.

"Remember, this was your choice," Deacon said as he bent down behind the soldier's chair. His arms were secured to the metal back and James felt that giddy rush of adrenaline as he watched his brother. Once again he felt that slight pang of envy in his chest— Deacon was having all of the fun.

The soldier yelled through clenched teeth, small beads of spit spraying from his mouth as Deacon pulled one fingernail from the man's hand. The soldier slumped forward, panting like he'd just finished a half-marathon.

Deacon moved back into position in front of the man. He held out the pliers so the soldier could see his bloody fingernail. *"How many would you like to lose tonight?"*

"Fuck you!"

"As you please," Deacon said, moving into position to extract another fingernail.

James grinned—insulting Deacon was a mistake, and he wasn't surprised when his brother took two fingernails off in a row.

The soldier's head dropped like he was unconscious. Deacon slapped his face, waking him up again.

"Who do you work for?" Deacon repeated.

"No," the soldier mumbled, not lifting his eyes.

Deacon tilted his head to the side. *"Perhaps this will change your mind,"* he said, changing tactics as he pulled out James's favorite weapon: the scalpel. It caught the soldier's attention.

Deacon ran this thumb over the edge of the blade for effect and the soldier sat upright again, suddenly awake.

"Care to curse at me again?"

The soldier was mute.

"*Who do you work for?*"

Deacon waited patiently, much more patiently than James would've. But when his brother sighed, James watched on eagerly as he tried to guess which body part Deacon was going to mutilate. He went for the right earlobe.

The soldier howled, his screams protected in the soundproof cell.

Blood ran down the soldier's neck, soaking into the cotton of his T-shirt.

"*He is not worth this,*" the soldier said through gritted teeth. "*What do you want to know?*"

Deacon had cracked him.

"*Who you are working for, and what do you want with Makaela Ashwood?*" Deacon asked.

The soldier cursed. "*Who knew she would be so much fucking trouble . . . This was supposed to be an easy job.*" He shook his head. "*I'll tell you what you want to know, but I want to know something in return.*"

"*You're not in a position to be making deals,*" Deacon said, raising one eyebrow.

"*I think you'll agree to the deal, because in the end you're going to kill me anyway, right?*"

"*That's right,*" Deacon said.

"*So tell me who you are. And I want to know how Makaela Ashwood is managing to pay you if it's not from her bank account.*"

"Samuel," James said.

"*I'm looking into it,*" Samuel responded.

James didn't like that bit of information at all. If they'd hacked into Mak's bank accounts, Samuel should've picked it up.

Deacon grinned. "*Okay, you have a deal. I'll answer both of your questions, but only once you've told me everything I want to know. Now, the sooner you start talking, the better.*"

The soldier looked to the wall, and then back to Deacon. He looked defeated. He knew he wasn't getting out of this alive and had smartly decided not to make his death any more painful.

"*Biskup,*" the soldier said. "*Alexandr Biskup.*"

James stilled—he knew the name. Alexandr Biskup operated one of Europe's most violent and profitable underground operations.

"And what does Biskup want with Makaela?"

The soldier blew out a frustrated breath. *"A code, apparently. He thinks she has a code that her dead husband gave her."*

James leaned forward.

"A code for what?" Deacon asked.

"I don't know. Biskup didn't say, and he's not the kind of man you ask. But, he's contracting men like me, and he's paying us huge sums of money. So whatever the code opens, or accesses, it must be very valuable."

"How much is he paying you for this job?"

"To deliver her alive—ten million dollars. Nothing if she's dead."

James cringed. Her husband hadn't just been up to his eyeballs in shit, he had been swimming in it.

"Interesting," Deacon said, twirling the scalpel in his hands again. *"I'm not sure if I believe you . . . that you don't know what the code is for."*

"I have no fucking idea," the soldier said, shaking his head. *"I was just doing a job, and being paid a lot of money to do it. When I accepted this contract, she had virtually no security. It was supposed to be an in-and-out kidnapping. But somehow you got involved and the game changed, didn't it? And when I realized her security had been stepped up, it was too late— Biskup doesn't accept resignation letters."*

The soldier looked pissed. And that was the problem with contracting in the underground world: sometimes the circumstances changed, but the job was still expected to be done.

"Why did you send her the notes?" Deacon asked.

The soldier's forehead creased as he looked at Deacon. *"We didn't. We assumed the Mafia was sending them."*

"What made you assume that?" Deacon asked.

"The trial. It was convenient timing for us because when we snatched her, fingers would be pointed straight at them. No one would even think to investigate otherwise. Except that's not how things worked out."

"And the ring?"

The soldier frowned. *"What ring?"*

James looked at their captive closely, and he didn't think he was lying.

"Move on," James instructed Deacon via their earpieces.

"*What do you know about her husband?*" Deacon asked.

"*Not much. I was still in the Special Forces unit when he was in Prague with Biskup. Rumor has it he was designing a software prototype for Biskup. That's all I know. Like I said, I was simply contracted to do a job.*"

"*And how many others have been contracted?*" Deacon asked.

"*Initially, four of us. But, as I'm sure you remember, you killed three of them a few nights ago. Well, I assume that was your group. New supports are landing tomorrow—five, I believe. My job tonight was just to assess the security, but obviously even I underestimated the resources dedicated to this woman.*"

"*What time are they expected to arrive? And where are they flying from?*" Deacon asked.

"*I don't know any of that, I was just advised supports will be here by noon tomorrow. You're going to have to figure that out yourself. Look, I've told you everything I know. Now fulfill your end of the deal, and then put a clean bullet in my chest and get this over with.*"

"No so fast," Deacon said. "Where have you been staying?"

"*In a safe house, on the corner of West Twenty-Second Street and Ninth Avenue. You enter from the shoe store on the ground level.*"

"*Is this where the supports will go?*"

"*No, each of us had our own location. It will be the same for the new supports,*" the soldier said.

Deacon stared him down but the man didn't flinch.

"*You referred to Eric as her 'dead' husband. What makes you think that?*"

"*Whispers on the street coinciding with Biskup's newfound interest in Makaela,*" the soldier said with one eyebrow raised.

"*Do you have a direct line to Biskup?*"

"*No. Biskup is behind this, but I've only dealt with men much further down the food chain in his enterprise. Are we done now?*"

"I think so," Deacon said. "And, because I'm a man of my word, I'll tell you what you want to know. My name is Deacon Thomas, and as to how

Mak is managing to pay us"—he smirked—"*I don't think we have received a dollar from her, but that's something you'd have to ask my brother about.*"

The soldier's eyes widened, but in one swift move Deacon drew his pistol and fired two shots in the soldier's chest. It was a merciful death—the soldier didn't even have time to react.

Deacon wiped a blood splatter from his hand, his eyes lingering on the dead man in front of him. "*Well, this case is taking a turn for the worse.*"

James agreed. "This is fucking bad. Last time I heard about Biskup he was in the business of human trafficking, and he was dabbling in nuclear weapons. Please tell me he's moved onto something else, Samuel."

Samuel cleared his throat. "*Hard to say. Looking at the CIA's files, they've been trying to get close to him—rather unsuccessfully. They've lost seven assets in the process, and Biskup's files have barely been updated in the past five years.*"

"*So the assets got fuck-all intel and lost their lives in the process,*" Deacon said. "*Excellent.*"

"Samuel, do they have an asset planted now?" James asked.

"*Yes. A woman by the name of Julia West.*"

"We need to find her. And we need to go back and see if Eric left any breadcrumbs for Mak—intentional or not," James said.

"*Contacting a CIA asset is a very bad idea, James,*" Deacon said.

"It's preferable to having a chat with Biskup," James said. Biskup was the kind of guy who would slit a waiter's throat for bringing the wrong drink. "Samuel, get a jet ready. I'm coming home."

11

MAK ASHWOOD

Mak's eyes fluttered groggily as she woke, vaguely aware she was no longer alone. When her blurred vision cleared, she looked into a pair of beautiful dark eyes.

"Hey," she said with a croaky voice.

A sexy smile formed on James's lips. "Surprise."

And what a surprise it was. He'd only called her once while he'd been away, and it was now . . . Thursday, Mak concluded, as she cleared the sleepy fog from her mind. One telephone call in five days —what had he been so busy doing?

"Surprise indeed," Mak said, looking at the alarm clock on the bedside table. It was two in the morning. "You've been quiet, Thomas."

"I've been busy, and it's hard to concentrate when I'm thinking of you. And when I'm working, I need to concentrate. I can't be making mistakes," he said, squeezing her hand.

Mak nodded—she could imagine his mistakes came with grave consequences. "Are you back for a while?"

"I don't know," James said. "I need to leave again in a week or so, but if things stay as they are, I'll be here until then."

James weaved his hands through her hair, guiding her lips to his.

He seemed to hesitate but then gave in and brought their mouths together. Mak closed her eyes, her heart racing.

James deepened the kiss.

He climbed on top of her and the weight of his body was comforting. His tongue wrapped around hers and a low moan slipped from her lips. A moan that seemed to turn him on more. His hips ground into hers, and despite their bodies being separated by the bedding, Mak could still feel how hard he was.

"I missed you," he muttered between kisses.

Mak had missed him too, more than she wanted to admit. And her body had certainly missed him. Her pelvis felt heavy with arousal, and her heart was beating rapidly.

"I missed you too. I'm glad you're back," Mak said, "for however long that might be."

James looked into her eyes. "It's for as long as I can be."

Mak nodded her head—she wasn't trying to make him feel guilty, and by the way his body was reacting to her, he certainly had missed her. But leaving, with no promise he would return, was a hard pill to swallow and it was going to take a while to get used to—if she ever could.

She lowered her hands to his ass, gripping it and pulling him close. She pushed the thoughts from her mind. He might leave again soon, but for now he was here, and Mak intended to make the most of it.

"Hang on," James said, disentangling their bodies. He stood up and pulled his sweater over his head, dropping it on the floor. He pushed the duvet off the bed and climbed back on top of her.

A sexy grin formed on his lips. "I feel like my body is always running at a thousand degrees when I'm around you. Even before we started this, every time I saw you I regretted wearing a sweater. You didn't notice, but I was always pushing my sleeves up or taking it off."

Mak bit her lip—she loved his confession. "Oh, I noticed you taking it off."

He raised one eyebrow.

"Your T-shirt rides up at the same time," Mak continued. "It's a very nice view."

"Well, thank you," he said with an arrogant smirk. He lifted her arms over her head, interlocking their fingers again. And when he kissed her he seemed less in control—needier—and Mak liked that. It was good for the ego to have a man like James Thomas hungry for you.

Mak kissed him back, and when she lifted her hips she heard him inhale sharply, but he didn't stop kissing her. He stretched out their arms and secured his legs over hers. Combined with his body weight, he'd restrained her, and when she tried to lift her hips again she failed. James let out a small chuckle as he kissed her neck.

"That's not fair," Mak said.

"I don't play by the rules," James said, his lips moving down to her collarbone.

She writhed in anticipation but he didn't go any lower—he wasn't taking this further.

"You're driving me crazy," Mak said.

He was grinning when his eyes met hers. "In a good way?"

In every way. Mak wriggled her hands, and he let them go. She cupped his face, drawing his lips closer. "Yes," she whispered, kissing him again.

James rolled onto his side, wrapping his arms around her waist and drawing her in. He kissed her shoulder, letting his lips linger there.

"We should get a few hours of sleep," he whispered.

With a body taut with arousal, Mak wondered how that was going to be possible. But, as they lay quietly together, she felt her eyes slowly close and remembered how easy it was to fall asleep in his arms.

Mak woke before her alarm, but found her bed empty. For a second she wondered if she'd imagined James waking her up in the middle of the night, but then she looked at the ruffled sheets and the closed bedroom door.

She stared at it for a minute as a plan hatched in her mind.

She silently slipped out of bed and put on a pair of socks. And then she moved toward the door, gently prying it open. Thankfully, it didn't creak or groan.

With the door open she heard his voice, but she couldn't make out his words. In her socks, she tiptoed down the tiny hallway, thankful for the small apartment, but stopped as she neared the kitchen.

"*I need to know for sure, Samuel; that's a risk I can't take.*"

Mak held her breath as she eavesdropped on his conversation.

"*Until I see a DNA match for myself, I won't believe it—you know as well as I do how easy it is to stage a death.*"

Mak's heart missed a beat—it was definitely not a conversation intended for her ears. *Who is he talking about? And is it that easy to stage a death?*

"*I agree . . . I don't know. I'll be part of Mak's security detail today, and then I'll come and see you afterward. Make Biskup's plant your top priority today. If we can't find her from here, I'll have to do it myself . . . Okay, thanks.*"

Mak quickly backed down the hallway, closing the door behind her, and jumped back into bed. She slipped off her socks, pushing the evidence to the end of the bed.

She didn't know if she should have stayed and listened, but it had sounded like the conversation was winding up and she couldn't get caught listening. *What will James Thomas do if he realizes I eavesdropped on his conversation? Will he be furious?* This was his company, his business, and it was confidential. But it seemed like Mak only got answers when she pieced the information together herself.

She thought again about the look that had transpired between Deacon and Cami a few nights ago. And the more she thought about it, the more Mak thought something was going on. It had to involve the ring or the mafia. The mafia was the most plausible explanation, but her instincts were leaning toward the ring. *If James knows some-*

thing about my husband's disappearance, will he tell me? Or will he lie to me?

Mak sighed. She was at a complete loss with no answers, but she was sure of one thing—she didn't feel guilty about listening in on his conversation, and she'd do it again if the opportunity arose.

The door opened and Mak slowly opened her eyes, like she'd just woken up. James closed the door behind him, his eyes assessing her. *Does he know?*

He climbed back into bed, resting his head on the pillow beside her.

"How long have you been awake?"

Mak shook her head softly. "I don't know, a few minutes. What were you doing?"

"Just taking a business call," he said, looking into her eyes. A small, almost sad smile formed on his lips. "It never stops, not in this industry."

"Don't you get tired of it? Of always having to be available? Of never being able to enjoy life?" Mak asked.

"I've never known anything different, and it's never bothered me, not until I met you. Now I see the kind of life that should've been possible, but not with my past. And I have to accept that. I've made my bed, as such, and these are the consequences. I'll make the best of it, but I will never be able to leave my past behind."

His past was the reason for all of his security measures, and the driving force for their negotiations.

"But you can still have a good life, you just have to be careful, right?" Mak asked.

"That's what I want."

It wasn't doubt Mak heard in his voice, but resignation—like he failed to believe that was possible. What had changed in the past week? Did he still think they could make it work? Was the offer of a relationship still on the table?

"James," Mak said, commanding his attention.

He returned his eyes to hers, but they were clear of any emotion. He was the calm and collected James Thomas.

"We'll see what happens. Life is very hard to predict," he said. "So, tell me what's been going on here without me. How are things at work now that the trial is over?"

They chatted quietly for another hour, their bodies twisted over each other like tangled vines. James was good company, one of the things she liked most about him.

"Did you hear I beat Deacon at Ping-Pong yesterday?" Mak asked, unable to hide her smile.

James laughed. "No, I didn't. In fact, I heard it was the other way around."

"What? Your brother is a liar!"

His eyes danced. "Deacon is a good liar when it suits him."

Mak smiled, but then fell silent and looked away.

So are you, James.

12

JAMES THOMAS

A shooting star raced across the sky and his eyes followed it, but his mind was turned inward. They had made it through another day unscathed, but Mak's case was becoming increasingly complicated, and having a guy like Biskup after her was not good.

James was expected in Samuel's office tonight, but he'd needed a few quiet minutes alone to think first—to process the events of the last few days. A lot had happened, yet he felt they were further from understanding what was truly going on.

James stretched out on the lounge chair, tucking his hands behind his head. He'd made a mistake this morning—he'd been careless with the telephone call he'd made in Mak's apartment. She'd been asleep when he'd exited the bedroom, but she definitely wasn't when he'd returned. And, in her haste to return to the bedroom, she'd left the door slightly ajar. It was barely noticeable—the latch wasn't fully in the cavity—but James had noticed it, and that certainly wasn't how he'd left it. He'd known then she had at some point left the bedroom and subsequently lied to him about her eavesdropping. Luckily, when Samuel had pulled the surveillance tape to check her movements, they discovered she'd only overheard the ending. It was enough that it would stimulate her brain, but not enough to explicitly reveal he'd been talking about her case. It was still a mistake, and one he'd never make again. He had to be more careful around a woman who was stealthy enough to slip on socks so he wouldn't hear her. James shook his head—he would've laughed if not for the gravity of her situation.

Samuel had been monitoring her activity all day, but so far she hadn't entered Biskup into an internet browser, nor had she done any other investigative work. James knew she was smarter than that—she knew she was being monitored, so she'd be looking for a work-around, some other way to access the information.

Leaving Samuel to monitor her every breath, James had spent the entire day as part of her security detail, assessing and monitoring to make sure they had every base covered. It had been an uneventful day, a relief after the past few days he'd had.

Immediately upon landing, he'd joined his brother and they'd gone to Mak's apartment and searched through everything she owned. They even searched the apartment Mak had been living in when she'd first come to them—the apartment she'd lived in with Eric—searching for any signs of wall cavities or lifted floorboards, but they hadn't been able to find anything, as James had predicted.

But why would Eric give her a code? And if they were to assume he did actually give it to her, how would that code be useful, unless she knew what it unlocked? James seriously doubted Mak knew the code, or anything related to this. She had no idea what her husband had been up to, so it was unlikely she was harboring a code for something that must be worth hundreds of millions of dollars, or had major destructive value.

But if Biskup hadn't sent her the notes, or placed the ring in her parents' house, who had?

Eric... What were you up to?

The incessant questions in his mind were giving James a headache and he sighed as he sat up, preparing to go to Samuel's office. His gut instincts had told him there was more to this case, but he would never have imagined it would progress to this level, and so quickly.

James descended the stairs to Samuel's office, meeting Deacon in the hallway. Cami was already seated at the table with Samuel when they entered.

"Any luck with the plant?" James asked Samuel.

Samuel shook his head. "No, but I'm continuing to work on it. Also—unfortunately—I didn't get anything useful from the soldier's cell phone."

Bad news on every account.

"What are everyone's thoughts on this code?"

"I don't like it," Samuel said. "And I can't figure out what he would achieve by giving it to her. If he's dead, what use is it for her to have the code?"

James had come up with one theory for that after his star-gazing. "He might have done it to buy her security, at least for a little while. Biskup obviously has good reason to think she has the code—which must have come from Eric, or someone very close to him. If Eric was alive but hiding from Biskup, he might've thought that Biskup was going to kill her to teach him a lesson. Biskup's known for doing that to his enemies. But he's not going to kill her immediately if she has something he needs, is he? Especially when it's something he can't get from her husband, because he's either dead or missing. Biskup can kidnap her and torture her, though. And I think that's his current plan."

"I know you're not going to like this," Deacon said to James, "because your feelings extend beyond business. But I think we need to talk to Mak about this."

"How would having the code help us, though?" Cami asked.

"It wouldn't," James said. "Not at this stage, at least. Until we know what it's for, the code is irrelevant. I don't think Mak is going to know the code, but she may be able to give us more information about what Eric was up to, and that may help us find out what the code is for."

Samuel leaned forward, resting his elbows on the table. "I know they had a seemingly distant relationship, but no one would take it well if they knew their partner had told them nothing but lies."

"This is business," Deacon said. "We have been one step behind the game on this entire case. Look, Eric is either dead or playing a very good game of hide-and-seek, so unless we get to Biskup himself, we're not going to find out what he wants that code for. And her case won't end until we know that and can subsequently eliminate it, so it's not a threat to her safety. Getting to Biskup could take years . . . There is a reason he has survived for so long, and penetrating his security is nearly impossible. The best thing we can do for Mak is to eliminate the threat, and she may be the only one who is able to help us."

Deacon was right. Telling her the truth about Eric's past would get her brain thinking about everything he ever told her. She might recall something valuable, something that's only stored in her head, something she might never recall otherwise because it didn't seem out of place or unusual at the time.

"I agree," James said. He didn't want to do this, but it was becoming inevitable. "And I think the sooner it's done, the better." James looked at his watch—it was after midnight. "Samuel, can you please check if she's awake?"

The screens flickered and pictures of her apartment filled each one. James could see her sitting in bed reading what looked like case notes.

"Turn it off," James said. "Cami, can you please go and get her and bring her in here?"

"Sure," Cami said, standing up.

She closed the door behind her, and Deacon spoke. "Do you want me to do it?"

"No," James said. "I'll brief her."

After a long wait, Cami returned with Mak beside her. Mak looked over Samuel's office with eyes full of wonder before she took a seat next to Cami.

James cleared his throat. "We need to talk about your case, because there's been a change in the direction of the investigation. Recent intelligence has confirmed that the person, or people, threatening you are not related to the mafia," James said, careful as to what he revealed.

Mak looked between them. "So, who is behind this?"

"A man named Biskup," James said, raising one eyebrow to reveal he knew about her eavesdropping.

Mak pressed her lips together but otherwise didn't respond.

"We interviewed someone a few days ago who informed us that Biskup wants something he thinks you have. A code," James said.

Mak looked as though she might laugh. "A code? A code for what?"

"We don't know," James said, "and that's why we've decided to update you on the progression of your case."

She looked at all of them again like she was missing something, and she was because James hadn't dropped the bomb yet.

"I really don't understand," Mak said. "I've never met a man named Biskup, and I have no idea what you're talking about."

"I know you don't," James said softly. "You've never met him, but it is possible that your husband had. Or at least they had mutual acquaintances. Based on the intelligence we have at this point, we're assuming Eric told someone he'd given you the code."

"Wait, who is Biskup?" Mak asked. "What does this man do? Is he a real estate developer, too?"

And here it is. "Biskup . . . is a main player in the underground world in Europe," he said carefully, because that was a nice way of describing Biskup. "His interests are not in real estate development, but then neither were your husband's, not directly, Mak. Eric was not completely honest with you, regarding his career. From what we've been able to garner, he was not developing real estate in foreign countries. It seems he developed a real estate software program and later sold it, but he himself was not involved in real estate."

Mak seemed to be turning this over in her mind, but she didn't look upset. "When did he sell the program?"

"About eighteen months before your wedding," James said.

"That's where the money came from? He said it was from a successful development," she said.

"No, the money came from the sale of the program. However, his movements since that sale are our primary concern," James continued, getting the conversation back on track.

Mak frowned. "Which were?"

"Biskup has an interest in nuclear weapons, Mak. We're assuming Eric shared this interest with him."

Mak's jaw dropped and her pupils dilated as she began to process the information. "Nuclear weapons? Eric was not—"

She suddenly stopped, as she presumably realized she couldn't vouch for him.

"I find that very hard to believe," she said instead.

"I know this is hard to hear," Deacon said. "It's never nice to know someone lied to you—even if it all happened years ago."

"What do you want me to say? I don't know anything, and I obviously had no idea who my husband was or what he had been doing," Mak said.

"We don't want you to say anything right now," James said. "You need time to process this, then all we want you to do is try and think of the past, anything that might seem unusual or out of place, now that you know what you do."

"I doubt I'm going to be of any use to you," Mak said.

"We're just asking you to try," James said.

"Fine," she said too quickly.

From James's peripheral vision, he saw his team look to him. "We'll talk more later."

Mak nodded as she stood to leave, her eyes not directly meeting James's.

Cami escorted Mak back to her apartment.

"Samuel, turn on the cameras." James watched patiently until he saw Mak enter and close the door behind her. She went into the kitchen, appearing to stare out of the window. "Okay, turn it off. Set an alarm if she opens the front door of the apartment."

"Done," Samuel said after typing a few words on his keyboard.

"Once Mak has processed that information, she's very likely going to have a lot of questions, and the fewer details we reveal the better,"

James said. "Everyone needs to be very careful about what is said from this point forward."

With their meeting effectively over, they went to their respective apartments for the night. James said goodbye to Deacon but stayed in his apartment for a few minutes.

There was only one place he wanted to be tonight.

13

MAK ASWHOOD

Mak stared at the long, rectangular white tiles that lined the kitchen wall.

Nuclear weapons? What were you mixed up in, Eric?

Mak was the first to admit she hadn't been a very attentive wife, but this was hard to swallow. It appeared she'd barely known the man she had called her husband. *I should've paid more attention to him. I should have paid some attention to him. Any attention.*

"Mak?"

She heard James calling out to her, and she wondered what he truly thought of the situation. He knew now the extent of her failure as a wife.

"I'm sorry," he said, and he genuinely sounded sorry.

Mak shrugged her shoulders, unable to meet his eyes. "I should've known, I suppose. I might've known had I'd paid more attention to him."

"You were young, Mak," James said.

"A lot of people get married young . . . I'm not sure that's a very good excuse," Mak said, resignation settling in her heart.

"It's a good enough excuse for me."

"I think if I'd spent more time with him, I would've seen through the lies."

"Probably. But that's well and truly in the past, and I don't think it does anyone any good to dwell on the past," James said, tucking his hands into his jeans, leaning against the refrigerator.

"You never dwell on the past?" Mak asked.

"No," James said. "Reflect, sure, but not dwell on it."

Mak thought she saw a hint of sadness in his eyes, but it was so brief she couldn't be sure.

"Why is this Biskup guy coming after me now? Eric has been gone for so long," Mak asked.

"We don't know," James said.

She stilled as she recalled the telephone conversation she'd overheard.

Until I see that DNA match for myself, I won't believe it—you know as well as I do how easy it is to stage a death. We need that confirmation.

Mak eyeballed James, studying his expression and how it changed when she asked her next question. "Is Eric dead?"

"Perhaps," he said, his eyes almost challenging her—he knew she was trying to read him. "The conversation you overheard this morning was in regard to your case. We don't have Eric's body, but the rumor is he's deceased. We're working on verifying, but it may take some time."

Everything seems to be taking its sweet time.

"Why did you hire the private investigator when Eric went missing?" James asked.

"The police couldn't give me any answers, so I thought I'd try and find him myself. I thought he'd met with foul play, and I wanted to find him… I wanted a body to bury. I certainly didn't think he was making friends with guys like Biskup or that he was messed up in some nuclear weapons business," Mak said, almost choking on the sigh that left her lips.

Mak looked down at her feet as another realization hit her. "He staged his disappearance, didn't he?" Mak asked, not even needing James to answer. She was no longer blind to the truth.

"I believe so." James walked toward her, his hands resting on her hips as he drew her into his arms.

"How long have you known all of this?" Mak asked.

"We received the information from this contact a few days ago, but we were trying to get more information about it before we spoke to you," James said.

"But when did you first realize that Eric had staged his disappearance?" Mak pressed.

"I didn't have anything concrete until a few days ago, Mak, and I'm not going to give you information based on assumptions—not information like that."

"You're not answering the question." She narrowed her eyes.

"I had my suspicions from the start, but I had no reason other than a gut feeling to base it on. When you've had time to process this, you need to look back on your relationship—now that you know what you do—and think about his behavior and the things he told you. It might not have seemed strange then, but it may now. Things he asked you to do, places he visited, any business trips he mentioned . . . anything you would question now."

"He's been gone for thirteen years," Mak said. "I can barely remember what I did two years ago, let alone what he was doing back then."

"You might be surprised . . . sometimes we store things in our subconscious without realizing it," he said softly.

He circled his arms around her, kissing the crown of her head.

Mak pressed her forehead against his chest. "I don't think I'm going to be much help."

"Let's take things one day at a time. Right now, I think the best thing you can do is get some sleep."

Mak slipped her arms under his shirt. He was warm again and Mak hoped she was the cause. "Where are you sleeping tonight?"

"With you, if that's what you want. If you want to be alone, that's also fine by me. It's your call," James said, tilting her chin up with his hand.

She rocked up onto her tiptoes, squeezing him tight. "I think you should stay."

"I was hoping you would say that," he said with a beautiful smile. "I do plan on sleeping, though, nothing else."

Mak was awake when James opened his eyes. He gave a sleepy moan, pulling her into his arms before closing his eyes again.

"What time is it?" he asked.

"Nearly six."

James opened his eyes again. "I should get up."

"I was going to call in sick today," Mak said. "I want to go to my apartment. If I look through his belongings, it might help me remember." Mak never called in sick, but she had finished a huge trial, so surely her boss was not going to care if she took one day off.

James wiggled his lips from side to side. "Okay, I'll organize it. We'll need additional security, though, so you'll need to give me a few minutes."

"That's fine," Mak said.

James kissed her forehead, his lips lingering. "Why don't you take a shower and eat breakfast, then I'll call you when the team is ready to leave."

"Thank you," she said, watching him as he got dressed.

He pulled his jeans on, and then his sweater, before kneeling on the bed. He gave her one last kiss before he left.

Mak pushed the duvet to her feet, resigned to face the reality of her past. She had failed as a wife, but now she was determined to find out what she could about Eric and what he'd been doing. Searching through his belongings seemed like the logical starting point. The only starting point she had.

She stripped, dropping her clothes onto the bathroom floor and stepping under the shower. The warm water felt good against her skin and she didn't rush, knowing James needed time to organize the team.

Eventually she stepped out and dried herself off. She put on a light layer of makeup, tousled her hair into a ponytail and dressed in jeans and a sweater. She picked up her cell phone, and a worm of guilt burrowed into her conscience; she hated calling in sick, but she also felt she needed to do this. She made the call to her boss, put some bread in the toaster, and waited impatiently for James's call.

Mak turned her attention inwards as she warmed her hands over the elements. She couldn't remember the last time she'd gone through their personal items that dated back that far. She couldn't remember what she'd kept from those years. Of course, she had her wedding album, her wedding dress, and a few other photo albums, but had she kept anything else?

A knock sounded on the door, but Cami didn't wait for an answer before she walked in. "They're ready."

"Good," Mak said as the toast popped out of the toaster.

"Eat first," Cami said.

"It's fine, I'm not hungry anyway." Mak's appetite had a habit of disappearing when her mind was distracted.

Cami gave a disapproving frown but escorted her to the car park without another word. There were four cars in the morning entourage.

When they arrived at her apartment, Thomas Security followed their usual protocols of ushering her in. Once they were inside, she noticed James stayed by the door and Deacon took a posting at the window. There were ten other security team members in the apartment, but Mak ignored them as she looked at the tower of boxes. She suddenly felt overwhelmed.

Mak stepped toward the box closest to her. It was labeled *Kitchen*. She doubted that box held any revelations, but she knew which ones might—the boxes labeled *Eric*.

She found one sitting on top of another box, and when she reached for it Cami appeared by her side, helping her lift it down. Cami pulled a pocketknife from her jeans and Mak raised one eyebrow.

Cami shrugged her shoulders. "You never know when it might come in handy."

Cami sliced through the tape and stepped away, leaving Mak to open up the box.

Tentatively, Mak opened the flaps and began to sort through its contents. She pulled out a few items of clothing Mak remembered had been his favorites. It seemed ridiculous she'd kept them all these years, but at the time she had originally sorted through his belongings—about five years after he'd gone missing and she knew he wasn't coming back—it had seemed too cruel to throw everything away, completely extinguishing his life.

She found the gold watch she remembered had been his grandfather's. She turned it over, ran her thumb over the back, and put it aside with his clothing. The rest of the box was filled with much of the same, and once she'd reached the bottom of it, she repacked everything and moved on to the next box. And then the next. And then the next.

"Mak, do you want something to eat?" Cami was beside her again, helping her lift another box.

Mak checked her watch; she'd lost track of time. The morning was almost over and her efforts were proving fruitless, which irritated her.

"No, I'm fine, thanks," Mak said.

Cami didn't respond, but a few seconds later Mak overheard her giving coffee orders. ". . . and Mak will have a strong latte." Someone exited the apartment, presumably to get the coffees, but Mak continued her search. The next box was labeled *Office*.

Mak picked up Cami's pocketknife and slit it open. She immediately recognized the portfolio folders as Eric's. Mak opened one of them and looked at the first page—it was a picture of a multi-story development. She recalled a memory of him telling her about it and how excited he'd been. It was a big development, the one he had been working on when he disappeared.

Mak flicked through the pages, her eyes scanning over the floor plans, materials, and costings.

"James?" Mak called, not looking up from the folder.

She smelled his cologne as he approached her.

"Yes," he said.

"Look at this." Mak gave him the folder. "Look at the details in this folder. Why would he have all of this if he wasn't developing real estate?" Mak pulled out more and more portfolio folders, each one dedicated to a different development.

"It could be Eric had these as research for his software program, which was created specifically for real-estate developers. He would need this kind of information in order to build such a program."

"Why would he need to lie about it? Why not tell me he was developing a program? Why would I care?"

"Because I think telling you and everyone around him he was developing real estate in foreign countries gave him a good excuse to travel, and no real opportunity for people to check on him—especially once he'd sold the software program. It eliminated the risk of anyone happening to go by the development and realize he wasn't actually working there when no one knew him. By keeping it in the same industry, he had the knowledge to back up his lies."

"A weekend in Ukraine wasn't high on my agenda," Mak muttered.

"Ukraine? Was he developing in Ukraine?"

Mak looked at the folder in her hands, checking the location of the development: Greece. When had he been developing in Greece?

She checked the dates of the developments, because maybe she was getting them confused—it was a long time ago.

She pulled out all of the portfolio folders—the developments were scattered across Europe, but none of them in Ukraine. But he had definitely been there.

"Mak?" James repeated.

"Maybe he traveled through there on one of his trips," Mak said, but even as she said it aloud it seemed unlikely he would stop for some sightseeing in Ukraine on the way to or from one of his developments.

"What makes you think he was in Ukraine?" James asked.

"I don't think it, I know he was. He had become quite distant at one point, and I thought maybe he was having an affair, so I went through his phone and his bag when he got home. I didn't find anything except a few photographs of him, with another guy I didn't know, in front of St. Michael's Cathedral—you know, the big blue one with the gold tops."

"You know that cathedral?" James asked.

"Strangely a few weeks earlier I'd been watching a documentary on television about some of the most amazing cathedrals in the world. It was profiled on the show, otherwise I wouldn't have had a clue. But he was standing in front of it—a tourist shot."

"When was this?" James asked.

Mak searched through her memories. "I don't know, but before we got married . . . so, maybe sixteen years ago."

"And you didn't recognize the guy?"

"No, but I don't think I paid much attention to him because I didn't care if Eric was there with another guy—I think I just assumed it was someone he was working with. I don't know why I didn't think it was strange he was in Ukraine, though . . . I'm sure he told me he was working there, and then I found the photographs when he got back and thought nothing more of it," Mak said, her voice as distant as her memories.

"That makes sense," James said, taking the folder back from her.

"Or just empty rationale," Mak said, moving on to the next box.

The box that would change everything.

14

JAMES THOMAS

What were you doing in Ukraine, Eric?

That nugget of information had come as a total surprise. James didn't know how helpful it would be, but that was the thing about intelligence work: sometimes the smallest detail was the key to solving the case.

James continued to watch Mak, monitoring her reactions and expressions to the items she found. He already knew what was in the boxes—he'd been through them all a few days ago—but something that appeared normal to him could be completely abnormal to Mak. And as James continued to watch her, he knew they'd made the right decision in telling her about her husband's lies.

The coffee arrived, as did the food Deacon had taken the liberty of ordering. His staff changed shifts, giving some of the guys a break to eat, while others continued to monitor and survey the environment. James didn't particularly like being here—a known, prior location of Mak's—but he had ample guys to protect her if they were ambushed.

James took Mak's coffee to her. He wasn't sure she'd take it, but she did. She took one sip and put it down next to the box. When Mak Ashwood was focused, she was focused. James was interested to see her reactions to this box—particularly the old photographs of them together. James did feel a little guilty he and his brother had searched her entire life belongings, but they'd done it with her best interests in mind. They'd also done it to many other clients, and he'd never felt any guilt in the past, but everything was different with her. He didn't want to intrude on her life, but he also had to treat her like a client as much as possible in order to resolve her security situation—and that meant collecting his own intelligence his way.

James studied her face as she opened the box. She showed very little emotion, and he didn't know if it was because she knew she was surrounded by his security team, or if it was because so much time had passed that her emotions had been buried long ago with any hope of finding him.

Mak put the selection of photographs back in the shoebox with the others, but she didn't put it in the larger box, instead she placed it beside her coffee. She continued searching through the large box, pulling out and putting back items after she reviewed them. She pulled out a navy suede jewelry pouch, scrunching her small nose as she tipped a gold locket into the palm of her hand.

She opened the locket and tilted her head, examining it like a foreign object.

"Strange," she muttered, giving a slight shake of her head.

"What is strange?" James asked, moving toward her.

"That locket," she said. "I don't remember it. And it has a photo of me, which doesn't seem like him—he wasn't exactly the romantic type. I don't think I've seen it before, but I guess I must've considering that I packed these boxes," she said.

James held out his hand, and she passed him the locket. He looked over it much more closely than he had a few days ago. The front of it was engraved with a floral design and a symbol in the middle. James stared at it, and the longer he did his instincts told him not to ignore it. It looked like any ordinary locket, but the fact that Mak didn't think she'd ever seen it was strange. James opened it and pulled out the plastic and the photograph, turning it over but the back of the paper was blank. He checked the locket for any inscriptions but he couldn't see any. While Mak was preoccupied, he slipped the locket into his pocket and then put the fabric pouch back into the box. She lifted her eyes enough to register his movement but continued on with her search.

James noticed his brother watching him with interest, and a few minutes later James excused himself into the hallway. He took the locket out of his pocket and held it in the palm of his hand as he took a photo on his cell phone. Deacon came through the door just as he was sending the photograph to Samuel.

"What's up?" Deacon said, taking the locket.

"I don't know," James said, frowning. "Look at that symbol in the middle. Does it look even vaguely familiar to you?"

Deacon looked at it silently for a few seconds. "No, not at all. Is it familiar to you?"

"I don't know . . . I feel like maybe I've seen it before, but it's a very vague feeling. I've sent a photograph to Samuel to see if he can match it to anything," James said.

Deacon shrugged his shoulders. "Wait and see," he said, going back into the room.

James took a minute longer, staring once more at the locket before he put it into his pocket and went back to work.

The sun had set and the bitter-cold night had settled in before Mak finished looking through her boxes. They found one definitive piece of information today: Eric had spent some time at least in Ukraine. And another possible piece: the locket, although Samuel had yet to come back with any confirmation.

James peered out the window, watching the street. He was eager to get back to the safety of Thomas Security, but he waited patiently as Mak repacked the final items into the box and picked up the shoebox she'd set aside earlier, cradling it in one arm.

James didn't mention it but simply asked if she was ready to go. She nodded her head, and he noted how tired she looked—not helped by the fact that she hadn't eaten all day, and he didn't think she'd slept much last night.

James and Cami flanked Mak as they exited the building. They were on high alert after spending the entire day in the apartment, but they arrived back at their headquarters uneventfully.

"You should eat," Deacon said to Mak as they rode the elevator to their apartments.

"I think we should all eat—a picnic on the rooftop," Cami said.

Mak didn't look too eager and her eyes flickered to James, but if she thought he was going to help her weasel her way out of dinner, she was very wrong.

"I think that sounds like a great idea," James agreed.

Mak gave a slight roll of her eyes but otherwise didn't refuse. Deacon held his security pass to the elevator panel and bypassed all of the floors, taking them straight to the top.

It was rare that they invited clients into their personal spaces in this building, and they'd never had a client stay in the apartment for as long as Mak now had. That was James's doing, although not once had Deacon or Cami voiced their concerns about it.

They sat at the outdoor dining table on the rooftop, waiting for the food to arrive. James called Samuel and invited him up, but as usual Samuel didn't want to leave his office. He said he was busy looking into the symbol, and James didn't argue. As much as he loved Samuel's company, the harder he was working the better right now.

"Today was a long day for you," Deacon said to Mak.

"In some ways," Mak said. "I don't know what I was looking for. There was nothing there, except the project portfolios I suppose, that countered the life I thought he was living."

"The ones closest to us are the most capable of deceiving us," Deacon said. "They know us, they know our weaknesses and our strengths, and they know how to play us."

Mak didn't respond but tilted her head back to look at the stars.

"Anyway," Deacon said, "let's tell James about the Ping-Pong competition, and who really is the master."

A small, resistant grin formed on Mak's lips. "You're delusional."

"But I did win, right?" Deacon asked, beaming a smile at her.

"You cheated!" Mak said, warming to the conversation. It was a good distraction tactic by Deacon.

Deacon scoffed. "I did not! I won, and you can't handle it."

James chuckled as he saw the competitiveness blaze in Mak's eyes.

"You slammed the ball at me—an illegal shot! How can you say that isn't cheating? You, Deacon Thomas, were getting desperate because you knew you were going to lose."

Deacon threw his head back, laughing. "You missed the shot, Mak, and having your sister referee is biased, so that doesn't count. I think the only way to know for sure is to have a rematch. In fact," Deacon said with shining eyes, "let's play doubles after dinner. Me and Mak against you two," he said, pointing his finger between James and Cami.

James looked at Cami who nodded her head.

"Game on," she said, and James knew if there was a cheater in the group it was definitely Cami.

Mak looked at him, biting her lip, and in that moment he wanted nothing more than to taste it. James looked away quickly and when the food arrived, delivered by his assistant, he laid the spread on the table.

James waited for everyone to help themselves, and as he was spooning out his dinner, his phone vibrated.

"Hello," James said to Samuel.

"We've got a major, major problem. The money—Eric's money—it's gone. All of it."

15

JAMES THOMAS

James turned from the table, angling his back toward Mak.

"Gone?" James repeated.

"Gone. Vanished," Samuel said. "I can track it—"

"Wait a second," James said, pausing his conversation with Samuel. He could feel Mak's eyes on him and didn't need to look at her to know they were narrowed and watching.

James turned and pointed his finger at his brother. "Don't you dare start Ping-Pong until I get back." James then excused himself from the table.

He held his phone to his ear but waited until he was at the door before he continued his conversation with Samuel.

"I'm on my way down," James said, his voice echoing through the stairwell. "Are all of the bank accounts empty?"

"Every single one," Samuel said.

"Can you see where it has gone?"

"Not yet, because I wanted to talk to you about that first. If I track this money, I can conceal my identity so nothing links back to us, but depending on who is looking at this, I might not be able to hide the fact that I'm tracking it. Someone as good as me would be able to find the trace. I think it's unlikely that that's what we're dealing with here, but look at Jayce Tohmatsu's case—anything is possible."

James exited the stairwell, thinking it through as he walked briskly to Samuel's office. He ended the call as he opened the door.

"What was your first thought when you realized the money had been moved?" James asked. "What was the first rationale that popped into your head?"

"I thought someone was playing a game," Samuel said, pushing his glasses up the bridge of his nose.

James nodded in agreement. "I think whoever sent her the notes, and whoever placed the ring, and whoever is shifting this money, is testing us. At first I thought it was a message aimed at Mak, but I think it has been about us the entire time. Or rather, her security the entire time. The question is: who?"

Samuel tapped his finger against his chin as he thought silently. "I think you're right. But I don't know who else would have an interest in her besides her husband. And at this point we're assuming he is dead."

"Right. But what about one of Biskup's enemies? I'm sure he's made plenty of them. I'm starting to think more about Eric; I'm thinking he created something for Biskup, but perhaps Eric got greedy. Or perhaps Biskup changed the terms and conditions of the deal, and Eric didn't like it anymore. Maybe he went to someone, one of Biskup's rivals, with the prototype, or whatever his business was. Maybe this person also knows about the code. And if they are testing her security, they are doing it to either find a hole in our system to penetrate it to get her, or, if they think we're doing a satisfactory job protecting her, they might let us continue for the time being. I mean, if we took out Biskup, it would solve one huge problem for them, right?"

Samuel nodded confidently. "So, what do we do? Do you want to show them our cards, or do you want them to underestimate us?"

James leaned back in the chair, folding his hands behind his head. "I think we should show them our cards this time. If they think we're not capable of protecting her, they might decide to come for her. Or, if they are trying to find our weakness, they're going to come for her regardless, so it doesn't really matter. We've got Biskup's guys to deal with right now, and I'd prefer to clean up that mess before we get embroiled in another."

"I agree," Samuel said. "Ready?"

James nodded his head and Samuel projected his laptop screen onto one of the large screens on the wall. James watched as Samuel entered a series of codes. Several suspenseful minutes passed, and then Samuel paused, pulling his lips to the side. James looked at the screen as Samuel tapped one last button. The details of a bank account displayed. They had moved the money into Mak Ashwood's bank account.

"Move it out," James said. There were several reasons why he didn't want that money in there—first and foremost because it made her even more of a target.

"Eric's feeling rather charitable tonight," Samuel said with a crooked smile. He transferred the money into six different charity organizations and then doctored the bank records so Mak would never see the transactions. "Now we wait and see who we're really playing with. If they can undo my work, we've got a real problem," Samuel said.

Back to the waiting game.

"Where are we at with my case?" James asked. He felt like he'd barely had time to think about anything other than Mak since he'd returned.

"I have a team monitoring every conversation Mr. Roberts is having, either from his office in the Docoss Hotel or from his home. He's done nothing out of the ordinary, nor has he had any dealings with anyone suspect. A few days after your visit his nerves seemed to settle down, probably once he convinced himself you're not coming back—for a few weeks at least. Other than that, we really don't have any new leads. You'll need to be at that party, though."

James did have to be there, but he'd like Mak's case to be a little more stable before he left in a few days.

"Where are we at with the occult investigations? I know we

discussed them after my conversation with Dasha, but I'm assuming nothing new has come of that."

Samuel sighed. "Correct, unfortunately. The guys have been researching the three groups we identified, and we can't make a connection with any of the known Escanta associates. The problem is, we might be looking for the wrong connections. They might be connected to the next layer, or even higher. The occult practices Dasha mentioned were referenced to the main group, the years-old underground group. And we don't know who any of them are."

Samuel paused, typing on his keyboard, and then continued.

"We did look into the numerological significance of the number six—the number the Romanian group likes to carve into the chests of their victims. Of all numbers, six seems to be the most spiritual number. Many sacred geometrical symbols, such as the Star of David, have six points. It's regarded to be a powerful and unique number, and many spiritual sites will reference that seeing a number 'six' is a message from the angels to balance material and spiritual goals. We haven't been able to find anything disturbing, as such, although I guess if some crazed being wanted to, he could radicalize it any way he wanted for his own benefit."

"We see that every day," James muttered in agreement. "Any luck with the symbol on the locket?"

"No, but considering you've only given me a few hours, what did you expect?"

James grinned. "I think there's nothing you can't do, Samuel."

Samuel scoffed. "Sometimes I wonder . . ."

James's phone vibrated and he answered it, putting it on speaker. "Deacon."

"We're about ready to play Ping-Pong."

James looked to Samuel, who shrugged his shoulders in response and James knew what he was thinking—it could be a long waiting game. Forever, maybe. Hopefully.

"I'll meet you there," James said, standing up. He slipped the phone back into his pocket. "Do you want to join us?" James asked Samuel, already knowing his response.

Samuel laughed. "No, but I might watch you lose on my screen here."

James's mouth dropped into an *O*. "I am not going to lose."

"She's actually very good, and if she's teamed with Deacon . . . well, you better bring your *A game,* my friend."

"I will not let her beat me."

Samuel's eyes shone. "You might not have a say in it."

James walked out of Samuel's office, shaking his head in disbelief. Now that Samuel was evidently backing against him, he was more determined to win. And, as he reflected on the players that would be involved, he wondered if there existed more competitive individuals than the four of them. Maybe Jayce Tohmatsu—he really liked to win.

They were setting up when James entered the room and Mak's eyes flickered to him. He gave her a smile that indicated nothing of the stresses his mind was currently subjected to.

"All right, ready to win, Cami?" James asked, taking a paddle from her outstretched hand.

"Damn right, Thomas. Don't let me down."

James chuckled. Why did his team have no faith in him tonight?

He took his position at the end of the table, facing Mak. He could see the competitiveness in her eyes, and the thrill of the challenge. This should've been their date weeks ago, and although they were with company tonight, it was better than missing out altogether.

She raised one eyebrow and heat flooded his body.

Game time, baby.

16

MAK ASHWOOD

Mak's heart pounded in her chest, and her limbs tingled with excitement. His façade had dropped for a moment, and she'd seen the salaciousness in his eyes, and the heat. Who knew Ping-Pong could be such good foreplay?

Truthfully, an hour ago she hadn't been in the mood to play at all. But, as she stood opposite James now, there was nothing she'd rather be doing. And to beat him would be the icing on the cake.

Mak served first. Cami's reflexes were quick and the ball came hurtling back at her, but she didn't miss the shot. Nor did James, and he fired back a shot that wasn't unlike his cheating brother's.

"No!" Deacon yelled as he missed the shot.

"You're supposed to hit it!" Mak exclaimed.

"And you're supposed to be a supportive team member," Deacon said.

James and Cami laughed at the other end, and Mak's concentration lapsed because she missed her next shot.

"Time out," Deacon said.

"No way," James said. "We've been playing for all of four minutes. No time out."

Deacon ignored him and whispered in Mak's ear. "We can do this. They're going to underestimate us now, so that's good. Let's win."

Mak held back laugher as she looked at him, because he seemed completely serious. "Go team," she said with a voice that matched his expression.

Mak and Deacon improved from there and an hour later they were still going at it back and forth. When Cami hit the winning shot Deacon banged his hands on the table.

"Fuck!"

James laughed loudly, but Mak kept her eyes on Deacon—she couldn't stand to see the gloating in James's eyes.

"Rematch tomorrow night," Deacon said, his fighting spirit still alive.

"You're on," James agreed.

Mak walked toward the cupboard to put their paddles away, and James snuck up behind her and whispered, "Who's the master?"

Mak's chest constricted, and she didn't dare turn around because she knew she wouldn't be able to hide the raging lust she felt inside. She put the paddles away, organizing them perfectly to buy time to collect herself, and when she finally turned around James was standing next to his brother, talking casually.

Mak covered her mouth as she yawned, and both brothers turned to look at her.

"Let's go," James said, leading the group toward the door. "Cami, can you please take Mak up and then meet us in Samuel's office?" James asked.

"I don't need someone to escort me back to my apartment. I'm more than capable of finding my own way, and it's not like anyone is going to attack me, right?" The notion of being escorted everywhere was beginning to drive Mak crazy.

"That's not what I'm worried about," James said. "I'm more concerned that you won't go back to your apartment, but rather do a little investigating of your own." James had that sexy, arrogant smirk on his lips.

"Unbelievable. Who told you about that? Nothing escapes you, does it?"

James didn't wipe the smile off of his face. "No, it doesn't."

Deacon laughed and Mak turned away from them, exiting the elevator, aware that Cami was following behind.

"Did you tell him?" Mak asked Cami while she unlocked her apartment door.

"No. I think Samuel might've, though. I think he thought it was quite hilarious," she said with a playful voice.

Mak bid Cami goodnight and entered her apartment. She locked the door behind her, although she doubted she needed to. She was probably just as safe sleeping with the door open, given how impenetrable this building appeared.

As she walked into the kitchen, her eyes landed on the box of photographs she'd brought over from her apartment. She considered whether or not to look at them but decided against it—she didn't want to get muddled in the past tonight. What she did want to do was take a long bath and go to bed. And she wanted to go back to her job in the morning—the job she loved more than anything—she would go on with her life. Eric had lied to her, their marriage had been a lie, but her career wasn't, nor was the life she had built for herself—that was all real. In time, maybe tomorrow, or maybe the day after, she would think more about her life with Eric, but not tonight.

Mak sat on the edge of the tub and turned on the tap, letting the water gush out. She scrolled through her phone while she waited for it to fill up, checking to see if she'd missed anything important at work. She hadn't. When the water level had risen halfway up, she picked up a bottle of bubble bath and poured a few drops in.

She tousled her hair into a high bun, stripped her clothes to the floor, and dipped her toes into the water, testing the temperature—it was a little warm, so she added cold water but didn't wait for the temperature to adjust. The hot water tingled her skin as she sank into the tub, letting the bubbles cover her shoulders.

The steam of the water and the lavender scented bubble bath relaxed every sense, and she closed her eyes.

When the water rose to her chin, she turned the tap off. It was a huge bathtub, much too big for her, so she pressed the sole of her foot against the tap to stop herself from sliding down.

This tub is probably big enough for James.

The thought popped into her mind from nowhere, and after his absence for a few days, Mak was glad he was back. She enjoyed his company and how easy he was to be around. His calm persona might irritate her at times, but it was also what she liked about him. He made every bad situation manageable, and she didn't believe she was the only one he had that influence on.

It was interesting to watch the interactions between James, Cami, and Deacon. And it was interesting to see how the dynamics changed when he wasn't there. The changes were subtle, but she'd seen them. When James was away, Cami and Deacon were a little more alert, a bit tenser. It was harder to see it with Deacon—and Mak thought he was much like his brother in that he was good at hiding his emotions —but Mak could definitely sense something different about him when James wasn't there. Mak knew her first assumption about them had been correct—the Thomas brothers might be co-owners of this business, but James was their leader. He called the shots, and Mak wondered why. Did James have more experience in his field? Was it his personality type? Or was it his apparent ability to stay calm under any situation?

Mak tapped her fingers on the wall tile, thinking about their relationship. Or the current status of it, at least.

James put no pressure on her to make a decision, and, as he'd told her, he'd never asked her to say yes either. But she knew neither of them could stay in this limbo. She'd gotten away with not making a decision for a few weeks now, but the fact that she was still living in Thomas Security was the reason for that.

The travel requirements. Her decision hinged on the travel requirements. Or, when you cut to the core of it, giving up some of her independence. She would get him in return, and the more she was getting to know him, the more appealing that was. She could imagine them together, building a life together—albeit an unusual one. As long as he was running Thomas Security, their schedules might be touch and go. But surely once her case settled down, they would have more stability. Jayce and Zahra had been in a similar situation, and now they lived a relatively normal life. Yes, Jayce had a bodyguard, and they didn't go anywhere without him, but otherwise they appeared to live their lives on their terms. Mak knew she would have more stringent security measures in place, but she was still confident they could carve out the life they wanted. And if her career continued to progress as it was, she might need full-time security for her own reasons anyway.

Mak sighed, stretching her neck from side to side, and sank into the water a little deeper. It was the most relaxed she'd felt in weeks.

"Mak?"

Mak heard a voice calling and her eyelids fluttered open. She looked down, realizing considerable time must have passed because there was very little foam on the water—leaving her naked body almost fully exposed.

She'd left the bathroom door open, and when James walked in he did a double-take.

She pressed her lips together, looking back at him. He was standing still, but his black eyes looked deeper than she'd ever seen them. Bottomless, like she was peering straight into his soul—and she liked what she saw: desire.

Small waves rocked back and forth when she sat up. "Can you please pass me a towel?" She didn't hide her body at all, nor was she embarrassed. She held his gaze.

He looked her over, seeming not to hear her question.

"Towel?" Mak repeated with a sly grin.

James appeared to break out of the trance he'd been captured in. He grabbed the closest towel and handed it to her. "I'll wait in the kitchen," he said, leaving before Mak had a chance to respond.

She smiled to herself—that had not been the purpose of having a long bath tonight, but it had definitely worked out well.

Mak draped the towel over her shoulders and climbed out of the tub, careful not to slip. She quickly dried her body and wrapped the towel around her torso, tucking one edge into her cleavage to secure it in place.

Mak walked into the kitchen and found James looking out of the window at the Manhattan skyline. He turned around before she said anything, the look in his eyes much the same as it had been in the bathroom, but he didn't move toward her. She waited a moment, assessing his body language, and walked toward him. It seemed like the entire universe was silent; all Mak could hear was her wildly beating heart.

She stopped in front of him, and he still didn't move, but when she tilted her chin up his mouth found hers, consuming it.

James groaned as he drew her in closer, pressing her body against his. His fingers tangled in her wet hair, pulling it, but the sharp pain only turned her on more. She stood on her tiptoes, and James lifted her, setting her on the edge of the tabletop.

As she wrapped her arms around his neck her towel unraveled, exposing her breasts. James's hands immediately found their way to them, then he stopped suddenly. He looked away as his lungs seemed to fight for air. Her chest felt the same—heaving and heavy.

He wrapped the towel back around her chest. "We can't do this; I can't do this."

"We can," Mak said, gently guiding his face back to hers. "It's okay, James, I accept," she said with a small smile. "I accept all of your crazy security measures. Or at least I'll try. I don't think it's going to be easy, but I still want to try. I haven't, however, changed my terms and conditions, and you can probably expect a few future negotiation sessions."

James grinned, but Mak could see what she thought to be hesitation in his eyes.

"What?" she asked.

He placed a small kiss on her lips. "I'm happy—I wanted you to say yes, I've always wanted that. But there is still a part of me that thinks this is a bad idea. You have to know, Mak, if I think I can't control any situation from my past, I will walk away, and that won't be negotiable."

Mak narrowed her eyes. "What's going on?"

"Nothing," James said. "But I need you to understand that."

Mak tried to read his face, to garner anything she could from him but he wasn't giving away anything. "Look, we're not talking about getting married tomorrow," Mak said, and he gave a small smile. "We're just going to try and date, right? We'll take things slow and see how it all goes."

He gave a sigh, and when he looked back to her, his eyes looked lighter, more playful. Perhaps his black eyes were the result of the stress in his life.

"Are you sure you want to do this?" James asked. "I'm serious about those travel arrangements, Mak, and they aren't negotiable."

"I know. And I'm agreeing to them, but remember your end of the deal: you're coming on an Ashwood family holiday, so really you're getting the crappy deal here."

He chuckled as he cradled her cheek in his hand.

Mak bit her lip as anticipation surged through her; she knew what would come next now that she had finally agreed.

James sucked on her lip and Mak closed her eyes, enjoying every sensation, every moment.

The tempo of their kisses had slowed, but the air was crackling with tension.

She tilted her head back as James's lips teased their way south. She held her breath as he unfastened the towel, letting it drop to her waist. He kissed the top of her cleavage, slowly making his way to her left nipple.

"Mak," James moaned as he took it in his mouth.

Her hands gripped his shoulders, and she wished his chest was naked. Hell, she wished he was naked.

She arched her back; heat shot down to her toes as his teeth gently grazed her sensitive skin. He moved to the other nipple, continuing to seduce her with alternating touches of pleasure and pain. James had once laughed when she'd asked if he'd enjoyed hurting people—maybe his thoughts hadn't been far from the bedroom.

"Take this off," Mak said, pulling at his T-shirt.

He straightened, allowing her to lift it over his head. Her eyes gazed over his lean body, and she felt another rush of arousal.

Mak wrapped her legs around his waist, pulling him closer. Their naked chests were flush, and every nerve in Mak's skin was firing.

His kisses were faster, and rougher, and his moans more guttural. "I want you so bad," James said as he sucked on her earlobe while Mak dug her nails into his biceps.

He elicited a groan, but it only seemed to fuel his hunger. James lifted Mak with one arm and discarded the towel with the other clothing. It was a swift move that seemed to require very little effort on his part. He always moved that way, effortlessly, and Mak knew it would also make him a great lover.

He set her back on the tabletop and kissed her again as his right hand slid between her legs. As his fingers brushed over her sex, she gasped, and her entire body tensed.

"James," she moaned, but he didn't stop, and she didn't want him to.

The pooling in her pelvis grew, and her breasts felt heavy and swollen. They had been teasing each other for weeks; it seemed impossible to control it anymore. Mak slipped her hand around his, reaching for his cock.

"I'm aching for you," he moaned into her mouth as he pushed his hips against her hand.

"I want to feel you," Mak said, reaching for the button of his jeans.

"Not here, we can't do this here," James said.

"What do you mean?" Mak asked as his fingers continued to caress her.

"Do you have a condom?" he asked, biting her lip.

Oh, damn, Mak thought. She'd forgotten all about that.

"No," she said, undoing his pants.

"We'll go upstairs"—he pushed two fingers inside her—"after I feel you come."

He looked into her eyes as he said those last words and Mak's body shuddered in response. His fingers began to thrust faster, and Mak knew he wasn't going to have to wait long to get his wish.

Mak brought her lips to his, kissing him with the intensity of her building orgasm. She moaned into his mouth, and when he pressed his thumb against her sex, her body erupted in delight; he muffled her screams with his mouth. Her body trembled in his arms, and she loved how attentive he was. As her body settled, so did the intensity of his kisses, as if in perfect harmony despite the yearning that must be consuming his veins. He opened his eyes and gave her that sexy smirk.

"We're going to have a lot of fun," he said with a slow nod.

Mak laughed softly, basking in the aftermath of her orgasm.

James grabbed her towel, wrapped it around her, and lifted her back into his arms. She wrapped her arms around his neck, and her legs around his waist, as he carried her to the door.

"No clothes?" Mak asked, a little alarmed.

"Trust me, you're not going to need any."

17

JAMES THOMAS

James juggled her in his arms as he exited the stairwell and unlocked his apartment. Her towel had slipped down to her waist, but he had no intention of covering her up and every intention of doing the opposite.

She bounced as he threw her onto his couch and drank in the sight of her small, naked body spread-eagled on the oversized cushion. Mak looked at him with hooded eyes, and James could barely believe this was happening—she was his, life had given him something he wanted so badly.

He held her gaze as he undid his jeans and stepped out of them. He kneeled on the edge of the cushion and grabbed her heels, sliding her toward him. James looked her body up and down, eager to explore every inch.

"Are you sure about this, Mak?" His voice came out quieter and lower than he'd intended.

She reached out her hand, taking his. "I'm positive," she said in raspy voice that hid none of her arousal. She lifted her lips to his, and his soul reveled in her touch.

James slid one hand under her lower back, arching her body into his. He had wanted this for so long, and he no longer had to hold back.

Their hands roamed over each other's bodies while their tongues moved in perfect sync. James lightly pinched her nipple, watching her face react. She moaned and tilted her head back—she enjoyed it. He caressed it, and then pinched it again, over and over again. She didn't tell him to stop, and as he slid his leg between hers, he could feel her wetness—Mak Ashwood was not averse to a little pleasure and pain. His fingers worked their way over her stomach, pinching and caressing as he continued to madly kiss her.

James was so absorbed in her, noticing every reaction and taking delight in every moan that slipped from her mouth, that he gasped when her hands wrapped around his throbbing cock. He closed his eyes, letting her pleasure him anyway she wanted. She was good and her fingers slid over his sensitive skin, stroking and twisting at just the right moments.

He buried his lips in the crook of her neck, nibbling on her skin as she continued to work him. His chest heaved, a thin sheen of sweat covering his skin. When he felt his orgasm building, he stopped her. He went to his bedroom and retrieved a condom from his bedside table, and then returned to the living room.

Mak surprised him when she held out her hand. He gave the condom to her, watching with delight but didn't expect what came next. She sat upright, put the condom between her teeth, and put it on his cock with her mouth. It was one of the sexiest things James had ever seen, especially because it was so unexpected.

"And for that you will be rewarded," James said as he laid her on the couch. He hovered with his cock at her entrance, and then pushed into her.

Mak inhaled sharply, and he paused. She was tight, very tight.

He weaved their fingers together, holding them over her head. "Are you okay?"

"Yes," she said quickly. "You're just . . . larger than normal."

James couldn't help the grin that formed on his lips, and she gave a slight roll of her eyes. He moved again, slower now, giving her body time to stretch around him. As her body relaxed, he moved his hips faster, penetrating deeper.

"You feel so good," James whispered into her ear.

Mak moaned as her panting grew heavier and heavier with each thrust.

He pulled her hair, tilting her chin to the ceiling, exposing her neck. She was restrained except for her legs, and he hadn't had to use any devices. Her breathy panting was beginning to drive him wild; he felt his control slipping. He pulled her hair tighter and she gasped.

"You like that, don't you?" James asked, pulling her into his arms. He turned around, sitting on the edge of the couch. She straddled him, wrapping her legs around him, pressing her heels into his back.

When she didn't answer, James yanked her hair, pulling her head back and tilting her chest forward.

"Yes," she said, her voice a cocktail of lust and pain. His favorite cocktail.

She ground her hips against him rhythmically.

"Oh, yes," she moaned.

James groaned, wrapping her in his arms. They moved together, kissing passionately. Mak's body began to tremble, and he let go of the last shred of self-control he'd been clinging to. He squeezed her ass, digging his nails into her flesh and she yelped, spasming around him. James swore as ecstasy flooded his body, and he entered a state of post-coital bliss.

James was breathing heavy and pulled back to look into her eyes. They were glistening, like stars shining in the night. Mak tightened her arms around his neck and laid her head on his shoulder. He kissed the crown of her head over and over.

Eventually, James separated them, mostly because he wanted to discard the condom. He lifted Mak and carried her into his bedroom. He laid her in his bed and pulled the duvet up to her chin. "Give me one second," he said.

He went into the bathroom and peeled off the condom, knotting the end, and threw it in the trash. He quickly cleaned himself, splashed some water on his face, and went back to Mak.

He climbed in and maneuvered her body so she was on top. He'd always liked how tiny she was, and how easy it was to lift her and hold her in his arms.

They kissed slowly, the mad rush of arousal no longer consuming their bodies and minds. Mak pulled back, leaning her forearms on his chest. He was bearing her full weight, but she was so light it didn't hurt at all, or even make him uncomfortable. It was just the opposite.

"You, James Thomas, are a very good lover," she said with a sly grin.

James couldn't help but smile. "Well, thank you," he said, chuckling. "And you, Mak Ashwood, just blew my mind."

She giggled, a sound he rarely heard from her. Yes, she laughed a lot, but rarely did she giggle like a young girl.

James laughed and then sighed happily. Right now, his life was perfect. He had everything he'd ever wanted, but he knew how hard he was going to have to fight to keep it—to keep this life he'd unintentionally built and to keep those he loved safe.

"Sit up for a second," James said.

Mak frowned, but did so anyway. James turned on the bedside lamp and looked over her body. He twisted her waist so he could see her back. She shrieked as she struggled to balance, but he had her safely in his arms.

"What are you doing?" Mak asked.

"Checking to make sure I didn't hurt you."

Mak's eyebrows creased inward, and she looked over her body. She was dotted in little red spots where he'd pinched her but James knew from his experience with torturing the human body none of them would bruise. Except perhaps the marks on her ass, where he'd dug his nails in, but so be it if they did.

She looked into his eyes. "The night you came to my apartment to insert the tracking device, I asked you if you like to inflict pain on others. You laughed and told me you do sometimes. Is this what you meant? Pain in the bedroom?"

"Not in isolation but, yes, I do like a little pain in the bedroom.

And that goes both ways," James said, wondering how she was going to respond to that.

She seemed to turn it over in her mind thoughtfully. "I guess I should've known that."

"Why should you have known?" James asked, interested to hear her thoughts, to see what she'd garnered about him without telling her.

"I think you get a thrill out of it." She looked deep into his eyes. "I'm right, aren't I? In and out of the bedroom you enjoy inflicting pain."

James debated whether or not to answer honestly. He decided on the truth, because she already assumed it anyway. "Yes." He noticed he subconsciously tensed his arms, holding her as if she might get up and run, but she didn't—she continued to stare into his eyes, looking for the answers he would never give her.

Her eyes flickered to the corner of the room and back again. "So, how far does this extend? Should I be prepared to be suspended from the ceiling and receive a good flogging?"

James cracked up laughing, and his whole body shook. No one could accuse Mak Ashwood of being indirect.

"I'm serious," Mak said.

"I know you are," James said, trying to control his laughter. "Look, I don't have a room set up for that kind of thing, nor do I have a closet of restraining devices—I'm more of a *use-what-you-have* kind of guy. I'm resourceful, I guess that comes from my past, but things like ties make for excellent restraining devices. And in terms of punishments, I like body contact—I like to use my hands. And I prefer to incorporate these things in sex, not create some elaborate scene and setup," James said, but then added, "unless you want that. If so, it could definitely be arranged."

Mak pinched his earlobe and scrunched his nose. "I think you should stick to your preferred methods."

James looked at the clock on his bedside table. There were only a few hours of night left, and while he wanted to spend those hours pleasuring her all over again, his sense of responsibility loomed larger. He had to protect this woman, and while he could perform on zero sleep—he'd done it before—he was definitely better with at least a few solid hours.

"Tomorrow night," James said, taking her bottom lip between his teeth. "Because we both need to work tomorrow, and I can't be half asleep on the job."

She gave him a look of understanding then settled beside him on the bed, tucking into the crook of his arm. He turned off the lamp, and the last thing James remembered before falling asleep was the sweet kiss she placed on his chest.

18

JAMES THOMAS

His alarm shrieked and James rolled over, turning it off. Mak moaned and pulled the duvet over her head. James pulled it back down.

"I assume you're going to work today, right?"

"Yes, I can't pull another sick day," she said without opening her eyes.

"Well then," James said, throwing the blankets to the end of his bed, "you better get up, because I set the alarm for as late as possible, and we don't have a lot of time."

Mak tucked her legs up to her chest. "You're annoying me," she said.

"I think you mean irritating," James said with a grin.

Mak chuckled. "I am actually sorry about that comment. I shouldn't have said that."

James kissed her. "Don't be. Everyone in my team thought it was hilarious. Even I laughed." Samuel had found it particularly hilarious and had stored that surveillance clip from the night they'd moved her into Thomas Security.

Mak tried to pull him on top of her, but James knew that was a bad idea, because he'd spend the next hour there. And he didn't have time, because in addition to getting in the shower, he had to go next door and speak to Deacon—and that was going to be an unpleasant conversation.

He got out of bed before his willpower diminished. James dressed himself in pajamas and pulled out a pair for Mak to wear. They would drown her small frame, but it was preferable over taking her downstairs in a towel. "Up," James said as he tossed the pajamas in her direction and realized how much he sounded like one of his old military commanders.

Mak sighed as she sat up, but a moment later she was dressed. She rolled the pants up so she didn't trip, and she was ready. James led her out of his apartment and back into hers. He kissed her goodbye at the door and then made his way back upstairs.

He knocked on Deacon's door but let himself in, as they all did at each other's apartments. Deacon was in the kitchen cooking, and based on the smell James knew it was eggs.

Deacon looked at him. "Should I make double?"

"Please," James said, looking at his watch. If they were going to talk, they might as well eat at the same time because otherwise he wasn't going to have time to do both.

James helped himself to a glass of juice, noticing his brother already had one.

"So, we need to talk," James said, and Deacon immediately looked annoyed. "I want to be honest with you, because I'm not going to, nor will I, hide anything from you. I know you won't like this, but I'm asking you to support me anyway."

Deacon pursed his lips and nodded his head, motioning for James to continue.

"Mak stayed with me last night," James said and Deacon squeezed his eyes shut. "I'm not going into this relationship lightly, Deacon. I gave Mak a stringent list of security measures she would have to agree with if we were going to have any form of a relationship, and she's agreed to them—at least for now," James said. "I want her, Deacon, I want her more than I have ever wanted anyone—"

"You're making a mistake," Deacon said with a tight voice, but

James knew his brother well enough to know he was making a huge effort to remain calm.

"I know what I'm doing, and I know the risks, which is why I insisted on her agreeing to all of these things before I took things further with her.

"You once asked me how I stayed so motivated when I had no life to live for, when my only purpose was to survive," James continued, watching his brother closely as he nodded in acknowledgement. "Well, I still don't have the answer to that, other than that is just who I am. But if you think I was motivated before, you have no idea how I feel now. I have this life in New York that we all share, and now I have her, and anyone that threatens that had better be prepared for the wrath I will bring to their lives.

"When I first considered a relationship with her I was worried I'd get distracted, and that would ultimately lead to a mistake. But I feel like exactly the opposite has happened—I'm prepared to fight for this life, no matter what it takes."

Deacon looked at him much the same way Mak had earlier, searching his eyes for the truth.

His brother sighed, rubbing his temples. "I don't know what you want me to say . . . I don't think this is a good idea."

"I'm not asking for your approval, Deacon, I just want you by my side for whatever comes our way," James said.

"Of course I will be, I just . . . God," Deacon said, shaking his head and turning his attention back to the eggs.

James didn't respond but instead gave his brother a moment to collect his thoughts and his temper.

Deacon placed the eggs onto two plates and put them down in front of James. He retrieved two sets of cutlery, handing one set to James as he sat on a stool beside him at the kitchen island.

"I've been thinking about the case after our debrief in Samuel's office last night," Deacon said, changing the subject, which was perfectly fine with James, because he had nothing else to say either. "I think you're right, I think the notes, the ring, and moving that money has actually been to test us."

James nodded his head. He'd given it a lot of thought after their debrief, too. He hadn't gone straight to Mak's apartment; he'd sat alone in his kitchen thinking through every detail of the case and the conclusion he'd come to was one he didn't like. He turned to Deacon, interested to see his reaction.

"I think he's alive, Deacon. I think Eric's alive," James said, and Deacon's eyes widened. "Think about the three scroll notes she received during the trial. *Death is but an illusion, as you will soon see.* I think that was him telling her he wasn't dead. *Keep your eyes open, Makaela.* He was telling her to be careful, because I think he knew Biskup's guys were watching her. *Contact, wait out.* That was for us, but it wasn't a threat from the enemy like we'd first assumed—it was a warning to help us get prepared. Again, it's as if he knows something is about to go down. And I think the subsequent ring episode and money moving are to test us. Placing the ring made it personal— I think it was a sign that he is watching over her."

"He's been gone for thirteen years, so why now?"

"Because Biskup's coming for her, maybe? I think Eric's probably been watching her—or had someone watching her—since the day he went missing. If Eric supposedly gave Mak this code, then Eric has the code, so he doesn't want anything from her—I don't think. But she was his wife, and whatever their relationship, I think he did care about her and ultimately he just wants her to be safe."

James took another bite of his omelet—Deacon was a good cook.

"So you don't think he's a threat to her?" Deacon asked.

"Not that I can see. I'm actually hoping he'll continue to help us. I think every sign, every note, every unusual event that happens, we need to look at it with an open mind and not immediately assume it's a threat. I do, however, think he's trying to work out who we are. Which, given our pasts, could be a problem because we don't know who he has made friends with."

"True," Deacon said thoughtfully.

"And because of that, we need to stay in the background. I'm going to leverage up Cami's support, but for the time being, until Samuel can find out more, I don't think either of us should be seen next to Mak. We don't know who is watching her, or even how they are watching."

"It's a shame we can't pull Lenny for this case," Deacon said, and James agreed.

They had promised Kyoji Tohmatsu that their best bodyguard—other than themselves and Cami—would always be assigned to Jayce, and would never be substituted. Lenny currently held that title. For James, keeping his word was one of the values he always upheld, no matter what, and so did Deacon, so Lenny wasn't an option.

"We'll move Tom up to Cami's first support. And we'll never be far away, just not by her side in public."

Deacon added, "I think we also need to create a decoy when we leave her office. We don't want to reveal this building."

James agreed as he ate the last of his eggs. He rinsed his plate and loaded it into the dishwasher before checking the time on his watch.

Deacon, who was already dressed, continued to casually finish his breakfast but nodded his head as James excused himself.

In his apartment, James went straight for the bathroom.

It could've been worse, James thought, as he lathered body wash over his chest. But he knew it could still get worse. Once it really settled in, their relationship could bring up the emotions Deacon had been suppressing for so long. The one thing James could count on, though, was for his brother to be a professional, and he would never let their disagreements get in the way of Mak's case.

James turned off the water, dried himself quickly, and dressed in his daily uniform. He checked his pistol, grabbed a bottle of water, and went to Samuel's office.

"Morning," he said as he walked in. Deacon and Cami were sitting at the table.

"Morning," Cami responded. "Mak wants to leave in thirty minutes. We were just discussing the decoy strategy for tonight."

James took the last remaining coffee and sat down next to Deacon, who proceeded to detail their plan.

"Good," James said, with nothing to add. "While we've got a minute, we need to talk about London. Obviously, I need to leave again soon"—James cleared his throat—"and everyone else needs to stay here to work on Mak's case, so—"

Deacon's eyes went wide. "You cannot go alone. We have no fucking idea what you're walking into at that party. There could be twenty guys there, and if Escanta has been hunting you, you can bet they know your face."

"I know that, so I've come up with another plan . . ." James looked between them all, not sure of the reactions that would follow. "I agree it would be foolish to walk into that party without any back up. I'm going to call in the favor from Haruki Tohmatsu. I want to take Haruto with me."

Deacon shook his head. "It's too early to call in that favor. I think we need to be saving it for when shit really hits the fan."

"No, let's call it in now and prevent shit from hitting the fan," James said.

"You're going to risk exposing yourself to Haruto, depending on what happens there," Deacon reminded him.

"I've given that some thought. But I did the same with Kyoji. He knew certain details of my past and never revealed them to anyone. Those boys might not live by a lot of values, but loyalty is one they do. And Haruto was as fiercely loyal to Kyoji as he now is to Haruki. Not to mention Haruto has known us by association for a long time, and he's a smart guy. He knew I had a background in intelligence," James said.

Samuel spoke for the first time. "James, Escanta knows you as Liam Smith. And now Joshua Hart. If they call you by one of those names, well . . . that's a detail I would really prefer Haruto not to know."

"It's a risk I have to take," James said.

Deacon rubbed his eyes. "I've been thinking about this all wrong," he said with a tinge of defeat. "I thought this relationship would get Mak killed, but she's not the one at risk, you are. You're already making decisions that are sacrificing your own safety—you're the one who's going to end up dead."

"No, I'm not. I told you this morning I have never been more motivated, and I wasn't lying. I'm going to get to the bottom of this. I'm going to peel back every layer of that organization and slaughter everyone at the top. And when it's done, I may move back onto the Russians and finish what I started there. I'm not prepared to walk away from this life—I'm not and I won't. The sooner everyone standing in my way realizes that, the better."

Cami looked at him the way she did at times: a mix of excitement and fear in her eyes, like she couldn't decide which way she wanted life to go.

"Okay," Deacon said. "Let's think this over for a few days and make a decision then—we still have some time to plan this."

Samuel nodded his head in agreement, but James had already made up his mind. He wanted Deacon and Cami here in New York, because he trusted no one more. And James wanted Haruto in London, because that bastard was as crazy at Kyoji Tohmatsu had been.

The games were over—it was war now.

19

MAK ASHWOOD

Mak sat at her desk, continuing her review of the legal case. She didn't like it, something wasn't right, and she wasn't convinced the man who had spent the past several years behind bars was guilty. In every case Mak had taken, she had been sure the defendants were guilty—that she was prosecuting the right person. But in this case she wasn't sure, and her distracted mind wasn't helping.

She'd spent a lot of time thinking about her failed relationship with Eric. She wondered how differently things might've turned out had she paid more attention to him and what he was really doing. She wanted to know what he was doing now—really wanted to know. But unless James could find the answers, she doubted she'd ever get them.

And there was the second major distraction: James Thomas. He was consuming more than his share of her thoughts, but those were much more pleasing, but naughty, thoughts. She'd expected to see him this morning but Cami had escorted her downstairs and into the car and James was not in sight. Mak assumed he had been in one of the other cars, but if he had been, he hadn't made his presence known. *And he still hasn't.*

Last night she'd witnessed what she found so attractive about him: other than his aesthetics, there was that combination of gentleness and hardness he blended so well. He was sweet, caring, and protective, but there was an edge to him—a hardness that couldn't be shaken. He made no apologies for who he was, and Mak liked that.

Her eyes flickered to Cami, who now sat permanently inside her office. It had taken some time to get used to, but somewhere in the process she'd managed to forget she was there most of the time. Which was helped by the fact that Cami was good at making herself invisible. Mak wasn't sure all bodyguards were like that, but Cami did it so well.

Mak closed the folder, acknowledging her mind was not where it needed to be tonight, and it was useless to stay late at the office. She hoped by leaving earlier, she might get more time with James.

Cami looked in Mak's direction as she tidied her desk. "Ready to go home?"

"*Home?*" Mak asked. "Where is my home at the moment, exactly?"

Cami smiled. "Temporary, Mak, it's all temporary. I know it might seem like this security situation is never going to end, but it always does. Life settles down, and this part of your life will become some hazy memory that, in a few years' time, will feel like forever ago."

"I hope so," Mak said, picking up her purse. She looked at the files sitting on her desk once more but decided not to take them with her —that was not what she wanted to be doing tonight. "Okay, I'm ready to go *home*."

Cami stood up, guarding the door until she was given confirmation that the team was ready.

"Does wearing that earpiece all day, every day, annoy you?" Mak asked.

"No, you get used to it quickly. In fact, I would feel naked without it now. Sometimes, though, Deacon's chatter drives me nuts." Cami smiled widely.

Mak grinned. "Did he hear that?"

Cami scrunched up her nose and nodded.

Mak chuckled and followed Cami out. Tom joined them, and they were all greeted by the waiting team in the lobby. Ushering her in and out of cars and buildings was another thing that had felt so foreign to her, but she'd quickly acclimated. She hoped it would be the same for all of James's requirements, but thought it unlikely.

They weaved through the streets of New York, but Mak paid no attention to where they were going. They were always detouring, taking different roads to get home.

Mak's head popped up, though, when the car stopped under a bridge. The change of cars was sudden yet swift. Mak, Tom, and Cami transferred into a waiting car before the other had seemed to stop completely.

"Evening."

Mak felt her pulse spike at the sound of James's voice. She cleared her throat, returning the greeting. Deacon was in the driver's seat as usual.

"Why do you never drive, James?" Mak asked.

He was seated directly in front of her, so she couldn't see his face. Mak watched Deacon instead, noting a slight grin form on his lips.

"Because Deacon is a much better driver than I am," James said, looking at his brother.

It was the same thing Cami told her when they'd first met: if you got into a car chase, you would want Deacon driving.

Deacon scoffed. "Infinitely better. James is a terrible driver."

"I am not."

Cami chuckled beside her.

"You are," Deacon said to his brother. "And don't laugh, Cami, you're not much better."

"You're a liar, Deacon Thomas. And if you stopped monopolizing the wheel, we'd all be much better drivers," Cami said.

Mak noticed that even when they were joking around, all of them were still alert—their eyes darting from point to point, their heads shifting subtly as they looked around.

Mak looked at Tom, who sat quietly beside her. She'd barely heard him speak, ever, but perhaps that was because Mak had never really engaged him in conversation.

"And you, Tom, are you a good driver?" Mak asked.

"Actually, I used to be a test driver in my former career," he said, surprising Mak.

"Really? How did you go from that to security?"

"Sometimes life has other plans for us," Tom said.

Mak studied his face, trying to read the man she knew so little about. In fact, she knew so little about everyone in this car, including James.

"In my next life, I'm coming back as a Formula One driver," Deacon said.

"In your next life?" Mak asked, chuckling.

"You're not a believer in the afterlife?" Deacon asked seriously.

"Well . . . no . . . but I haven't given it too much thought. You believe in the afterlife?" Mak asked.

"I do now," Deacon said, not taking his eyes off of the road.

"*Now*? What's that supposed to mean?" Mak queried, not letting him get away with that comment.

"It means that in this job you see some crazy things that will make you believe anything is possible," Deacon said.

Mak wished she could get inside their heads for even five minutes.

"You'll never be able to guess, Mak," Deacon said with a knowing grin.

"Maybe," Mak said, challenging his gaze in the rearview mirror.

His eyes creased at the corner as his smile deepened, but his gaze quickly returned to the road.

At Thomas Security, Tom said goodbye to them in the parking garage while they all loaded into the elevator. As per their routine, Mak was escorted to her apartment while a meeting took place in Samuel's office. It was the same every single night. She'd heard James mention debriefing a few times, and she assumed this was a necessary measure when they all spent so much time out of the actual office.

"I'll take Mak up," James said at the first stop.

Cami and Deacon didn't look surprised, and Mak wondered if James had told Deacon. If he had, Deacon had shown no signs of being against their relationship—but she knew better than to assume that was the truth.

As soon as the elevator doors closed, James pulled Mak into his arms and his mouth came crashing down on hers.

The elevator announced their arrival and he pulled back, taking her hands with dancing eyes. "Hello," he said.

Mak was startled by the passion in his kiss, and it took a few seconds to collect herself. He tugged her hand, and she followed him into her apartment. As soon as the door closed his lips were back on hers and his hands pulled her blouse from her skirt. His hands electrified her skin. They roamed over her midriff, leaving a tingling trail in their wake. He pushed her breasts together and moaned.

When he pulled back, he said, "How was your day?"

"How do you do that?"

"Do what?" James asked.

"Kiss me like that and then ask me how my day was so nonchalantly." Mak felt lightheaded and weak at the knees, and he looked none of those things.

James smirked. He grabbed her hand and held it to the hard bulge in his pants. "Still think I'm not affected?"

"Well, it's the only part of you showing it," Mak said.

"Believe me, I've been having thoughts about you all day. And most of them have been very dirty thoughts." His eyes blazed with heat, and they looked pure black.

Mak beamed a smile—that was the reaction she wanted from him.

"Are you going to Samuel's office tonight?" Mak asked.

He shook his head slowly. "No, I'm taking the night off. We're here so you can pack a change of clothes for tomorrow. And because I couldn't wait until we reached my apartment to kiss you."

"We're spending the entire evening together?" Mak had expected to see him tonight, but she didn't think she'd have dinner with him, too.

"Yes," he said, tapping her ass and moving her in the direction of the bedroom. "Pack for tomorrow because I want you for every available minute in the morning, and that includes showering . . ."

Mak's cheeks blushed and when she looked at him he gave her that sexy, arrogant smirk.

"Packing now," she said as she pulled a dress from the closet and practically ran into the bathroom, blindly throwing her toiletries into the bag. She was packed and standing in front of him within a minute. "Ready."

James chuckled as he took the bags from her hand. "Let's go," he said, once again leading the way up to his apartment.

Mak watched in amazement as he managed to complete the security passes on his door without putting down any of the items in his arms. He closed the door behind her, disappeared into the bedroom, and came back empty-handed.

James lifted her into his arms and set her on the kitchen tabletop. He kissed her slowly, but just as enthrallingly.

"If you're not working, does that mean Deacon knows about us?" Mak asked, studying his face.

"He does; I told him this morning," James said, tucking a lock of hair behind her ear.

"And what was his response, given your *no girlfriends* rule?"

"He's concerned, and he has a right to be. He knows I'm taking a huge risk by having a girlfriend, and he's worried about the consequences, and I can't blame him for that. I would voice the same apprehensions if the situation were reversed."

Mak cut to the chase. "He's not happy about it, then?"

"He's not thrilled, but you need to understand this isn't about you as such. This is about me being in a relationship, regardless of who it is. He likes you, Mak, he's just worried about the security risk."

Mak slipped her hands under James's sweater, her fingers trailing the lines of his muscles. "Is this going to cause problems between the two of you?" Mak had wondered about this before, but selfishly hadn't wanted to know the answer.

"Deacon will support me regardless of whether or not he agrees with my decision," James said, not directly answering her question.

Mak raised one eyebrow.

"He'll get used to it—I don't want you to give it another thought," James said, bringing his lips to hers. "And, I don't want to talk about my brother any more tonight, so please change the subject. Or talk less"—he chuckled—"either is fine with me."

Mak dropped the conversation and instead distracted her mind with the taste of his mouth and the intoxicating scent of his cologne. Her body craved him.

He grabbed her ass, sliding her forward so she balanced on the edge of the bench top. He grazed his fingers up her inner thighs, brushing over her already-wet panties.

"Good," he said and walked away.

Mak watched him, dumbfounded, as he retrieved a glass from the cupboard and walked to the refrigerator. He held the glass to the ice-maker panel and cubes tumbled out. He filled it halfway with water and returned in his usual calm state.

"Thirsty?" Mak asked.

He grinned slyly. "That's not for drinking."

Mak's entire body tingled as she waited for him to make his next move.

He held her gaze as he brought the glass to his lips and tipped one cube in. He swirled it around in his mouth and then tilted her chin up, holding it in place. Mak held her breath as she parted her lips, her body already wanton.

He kissed her with his icy tongue, holding her chin in place so she couldn't move; her body shuddered in response.

James undid her bra but didn't touch her breasts.

"Don't stop kissing me," he warned in a low voice that made her pelvis heavy.

She heeded his warning and kissed him passionately. She wanted to please him as much as he so obviously wanted to please her.

They continued making out, but the anticipation of what was to come next had Mak's mind in a flurry—she assumed it was all part of his tactics.

He drew out the suspense and then an ice-cold finger brushed over her nipple as she gasped into his mouth. She tried to pull back, but he held her chin in place, and she remembered his warning.

He kissed her harder, their mouths consumed with each other.

She gasped again when his icy fingers pinched her nipple. She moaned into his mouth and heard him groan in response.

"Lie back and close your eyes," he said, holding her head as he lowered her onto her back. "Good. Keep them closed."

His cold hands grabbed her inner thighs, spreading them wider, and she listened, trying to anticipate his next move. He pushed her skirt to her waist, and undid the buttons of her blouse, but otherwise left her fully dressed. The rough denim of his jeans brushed against the sensitive skin of her thighs, and she was surprised by how good it felt.

He took her hand, sucking on her fingers one by one and then dropped an ice cube onto her stomach. Mak tensed, and her eyes flung open. When he bit down on her finger she took it as a warning and closed them again.

His assault continued the same way, teasing her with sensation after sensation until she was a wriggling, moaning mess.

Oh, God, I'm going to come before he's even touched me.

His hand covered her eyes, and she felt him lean forward. In one swift move, he sucked hard on her nipple and thrust two fingers inside her; Mak spiraled into an orgasm—pure heaven.

"Fucking hell," James swore as he covered her stomach in tiny, feather-light kisses, her body still shaking. "That was so hot."

Mak was so overcome by her orgasm she couldn't formulate a response, nor could she instruct her body to move. Finally, James pulled her upright into his arms, kissing her gently.

She reached her hand down for his jeans, but he pulled back, shaking his head.

"No?" Mak asked.

"I'm all about delayed gratification—I like to be teased and made to wait. But don't worry, you're going to have plenty of time to pleasure me later," James whispered in her ear.

20

JAMES THOMAS

Mak sat beside him, her fork resting on her lower lip as she thought through her question.

"Stumped already?" James asked.

"Oh no, I have a ton of questions for you. But if I only get to ask one thing about you each week, I need to be strategic here," Mak said with challenging eyes.

"I see," James said, twirling another mouthful of pasta onto his fork, silently dreading the question to come. So far it had been the perfect night: foreplay, a cooking lesson, and good food. But this new development was not his idea of fun. He had agreed to it as part of her conditions of their relationship, though, so he wanted to uphold his end of the bargain. He could always lie to her, depending on what the question was, but James really didn't want to do that anymore than he had to.

"Okay," Mak said, "first things first; you only answered part of my question last time. You told me how old you were, but you didn't tell me your birth date. Let's start there."

"It's the 5th of January," James said. And that wasn't a lie, it was the actual birth date they used for *James Thomas*.

"Capricorn, huh? Make sense." Mak looked thoughtful again. "What is your real name?"

"I can't tell you that," James said truthfully—he didn't know his real birth name, and giving her the name Joshua Hart would put her at risk—there were more than a few men who would interrogate her for that name.

Her teeth dug into her bottom lip, obviously unimpressed by his answer, but his resolve didn't waver—he was not giving her that name.

"The night you took me to the hotel stocked with medical supplies you told me your favorite name was James Thomas. Why?"

"Because it's the name I use now, in this part of my life, and this is the happiest I've ever been. And . . . it's the name you call me."

A beautiful smile lit up her face. "Good answer, Thomas."

James chuckled. "I'm not lying—that's the honest-to-God truth."

A soft laugh flowed from her lips. "I'll take it," she said before consuming another mouthful of pasta.

"Now that I've upheld my end of our deal for this week, you know what you need to start doing tomorrow, right?"

Mak rolled her eyes. "You really know how to kill the mood, don't you?"

"It's important. After work you train with Cami in the gym, and then I'll take you for weapons training," James said.

"Fine," she mumbled, putting her fork down on the empty plate.

"And you're going to aim for the chest. If you continue to aim at the shoulder we're going to have a problem," James said.

"I will not take someone's life," Mak said.

"I appreciate that, and I love that about you, but you don't understand what it's like to be in a life-or-death situation. Sometimes you only get one shot, and if you were to shoot someone like me in the shoulder, depending on the penetration of the bullet, I could likely fire a bullet back. And if I couldn't, because I've trained myself to shoot both left- and right-handed I'd definitely be able to swap hands and put a bullet in the back of your head as you turned to run." It was blunt, but she needed to understand the consequences.

James continued, "I intend for you never to end up in that situation, obviously, but I can't do this if I can't train you to protect yourself."

"Fine," Mak responded, but James guessed, based on her too-quick response, she would aim for the chest in practice with every intention of aiming for the shoulder if she ended up in the situation. At least, if she aimed for the chest in practice, and she ended up in a real-life situation, her instincts would kick in and she would be more likely to shoot at the chest. That was one fact James was not going to tell her.

"On another note," Mak said, "when are we going to have a look at my potential apartment? It's fine staying here, but at some point I'll need to return to a normal life."

James stalled, deciding if now was the time to break the bad news. "I would like you to stay here for a few more weeks. I need to leave again, probably in a few days, and I would prefer you were here in this building while I'm gone. And—equally as important—I would like your case a little more stable before we move you into that apartment."

"How long do you intend to be gone this time?" Mak asked.

"Not long. A week at the most, I hope," James said.

Mak looked away, but James didn't miss the pain in her eyes.

"Mak?"

"This is going to be hard going forward because it's not like you're going on a normal business trip, is it?" She sighed. "I could fall in love with you and then the next week you might not come home and I would have to go through it all again . . ."

James slid her chair closer to him and cradled her face in his hands. "I can't promise that won't happen," he said. "But I can promise I'm not prepared to give up this life and I'd move heaven and earth to get back to New York if something went wrong."

"But that might not be enough."

"I know, but it's all I can give you. Even if I walked away from this job, from this company, it's my past that presents the most danger. That's something I can never leave behind."

The corner of her lips dipped down, and James knew what she was thinking: *Is this worth it? Is he worth it?* And he didn't blame her for thinking that.

Her lips were so close but James didn't want to kiss them, he didn't want to distract her mind for his own benefit. She had to answer these questions for herself, because the threat of his past was a life-long reality and would never change. Sure, he could eliminate some of his enemies and lower the risk, but he couldn't kill every person he'd pissed off—there were too many, and they all had friends.

"We'll see," she said finally and James nodded. He kissed her forehead, and then picked up their plates, taking them to the kitchen. He heard Mak's footsteps follow behind him.

"Tell me, do you have an ice-maker because you actually like ice in your drinks? Or is it purely for sex?" Mak asked, putting their glasses in the sink.

"Prior to you I haven't had women here, Mak. I would never bring someone back to this building for the security risk alone, not to mention how many questions the locks on my door would raise." James raised one eyebrow. "But, I can't say I picked out this fridge—I think Deacon actually did those selections—or that I regularly put ice in my drinks. I will say, though, I've never been more pleased I have one."

Mak bit her lip. "On that we agree. Does my future apartment have one?"

James grinned. "I don't know, but if it doesn't I will definitely get you one."

Mak laughed and James scooped her into his arms.

"I think it's time to finish what we started," James said, nibbling on her neck.

"Bedroom?"

"Couch."

Mak took his hand, leading him to the living room when his phone vibrated in his pocket. He knew it was important, because he'd specifically said he didn't want to be interrupted tonight. The message was from Samuel: *Our friend has arrived in London.*

A second ago his mind had been consumed with nothing but erotic thoughts of what he was going to do to the woman one pace ahead of him. And now he could think only of one thing: *Why had their friend arrived so early? What was he planning?*

James knew he had to leave tonight—he had to get to London as soon as possible. There was a chance their friend could've arrived on his own to make preparations, and if so, there was never going to be a better opportunity.

James texted a quick response, advising he would be done in an hour and to have a jet ready to leave.

James was reading Samuel's response when Mak turned to him.

"Bad news," James said. "I need to leave tonight, but not immediately."

Mak gave a small sigh. "When?"

"In a few hours . . . I want this night to go as much to plan as I had intended. I want to make the most of every minute with you," James said. *Because tomorrow is not guaranteed.*

"Can I leave the building while you're gone this time?" Mak asked.

"Just to and from work, and again that's nothing to do with us, but everything to do with your case."

She nodded and he took a step toward her. He put his hands on her ass and lifted her up so that they were at eye level.

Tonight, he wouldn't get to do everything he'd planned, but he would never take for granted that for the next hour she was his. And there was certainly nothing wrong with good ol' vanilla sex—sometimes there was nothing better. James closed his eyes as he kissed her.

She kissed him back slowly, but it didn't take long for energy to build between them, despite the circumstances of the evening. James lowered them onto the couch and once again untucked her blouse, but this time he took it off. He peeled her skirt to her ankles and threw it on the floor. She was left in her lingerie and heels and James hardened just looking at her. She wouldn't be wearing the lingerie for long, either, but she could definitely keep the heels on.

James sucked on the hollow of her collarbone, teasing and seducing her. She pulled his earlobes, and he felt the heat building in his body.

She started to undress him and he let her, his skin tingling at the touch of her soft fingertips. He lifted his hips so she could take off his pants. She didn't leave him with any underwear.

James returned to seducing her. He wanted to give her something to remember while he was gone.

Mak lifted her hips and moaned as he nibbled on her nipple. Never had a woman's moans sounded so erotic to his ears.

James ground his hips into hers, pressing her flat on the cushion. He kept his eyes open now, wanting to watch her.

His fingers brushed over her panties, and she shuddered. He pushed her panties aside and slipped his fingers into her steaming hot pussy.

"Oh, fuck," James said, his voice like gravel, and his penis throbbing.

She bucked her hips as he thrust his hands harder but his weight kept her relatively still. He enjoyed that minor sense of control, but regardless, he wanted his cock inside her—not his hands.

James grabbed a condom from a stash he'd left under a couch cushion, and as sexy as it had been when she'd put it on with her mouth, he didn't want to waste another second. He rolled it on, flipped her over onto her knees—which elicited a high-pitched squeal—and entered her from behind.

He gasped as he looked up at the ceiling, overwhelmed by the heat and tightness of her. He slowed until he felt her body relax, gently easing in and out of her. She lowered, leaning on her forearms, forming the perfect arch in her back. Their moans filled the apartment, and the low lighting projected shadows onto the bare wall. James pressed on her lower back, and Mak moaned his name. He pushed harder, tugging on her hair. She gasped, and when he felt her start to tremble he pulled out and flipped her over again. He lowered himself down into missionary and lifted her arms overhead, entwining their fingers. His mouth came crashing down on hers as he slid back into her. Their hips ground together, over and over, as their mouths consumed each other. James's chest burned from a lack of oxygen but it was the perfect blend of pleasure and pain.

Mak's body began to tremble again, and she tried to pull her hands free.

"No," James said. "Kiss me."

He didn't let her go, and he didn't stop either. She wriggled beneath him as her orgasm built, and when James knew she was on the edge, he let go. Heat and ecstasy shot to his toes as she tightened around him, finding her orgasm. Their screams were muffled by their mouths as they continued to kiss. When they became still once more, James let go of her hands and rolled onto his side, wrapping her up in his arms.

"I am coming back for more of that," he said, and kissed the crown of her head.

Mak laughed softly, and even though James couldn't see her eyes, he knew she was barely awake. He stroked her back, focusing on how amazing she felt in his arms. When he was confident she was asleep, he carried her into his bed, and tucked the blankets up under her chin without waking her.

He took a two-minute shower, packed, set the alarm on her phone, and kissed her goodbye—a kiss she would never remember.

21

JAMES THOMAS

Haruki Tohmatsu sat at his oversized desk, and James met his challenging gaze.

"So, you want to take Haruto as backup, but you're not going to tell me the details of this situation, correct?"

"Correct," James said without a moment of hesitation. He'd dealt with violent, power-wielding men for most of his life, and he was not intimidated by them.

After leaving his apartment, James had gone straight to the airport, boarded the jet, and made his way to Haruki's office upon landing in Tokyo. Haruki was going to make him negotiate this deal, but he was conveniently forgetting one thing—Haruki was the one who owed the favor.

"I'm interested to know why you wouldn't take your brother. Or Cami," he said, folding his hands on the desk.

"They need to be in New York."

Haruki raised his eyebrows. "Must be quite a situation if neither of them can leave."

James didn't offer any further details—he didn't feel obliged to, nor had Haruki actually asked him a question.

"Why Haruto? You're a resourceful man, James, why my son?"

Haruto wasn't actually Haruki's son, but like Kyoji, he'd raised him as if he were.

"Because your sons have a penchant for wielding weapons that I very much appreciate. They don't hesitate, they go in with guns blazing, and I've worked closely with Haruto before, so I trust him . . . as far as I trust anyone."

That earned a smile from Haruki.

"How long do you plan to be gone?" Haruki asked.

"Not long. A week, probably," James said. "The next five days will be critical, and I'll be able to provide a better update then."

Haruki looked deep into his eyes, and for a splinter of a second James saw a softness in him he rarely saw. He saw the love he had for his sons. Or at least some of them.

Haruki cleared his throat. "You can take Haruto, and two others of my clan. I lost one son too soon, and I do not want to lose another, so the more backup you have, the better. Not to mention, I would also like you to walk out of this alive—you're a *useful* person to know."

James grinned. "I appreciate it. When can they leave?"

Haruki picked up the phone, gave his orders in Japanese, and then put the receiver down.

"In an hour," Haruki said. "It's hard work, isn't it? Keeping your enemies at bay."

James knew Haruki Tohmatsu understood this better than anyone. And the fact that Haruki was still alive was a minor miracle.

"I do want one thing in return, though," Haruki said. "If I make it to my death bed, waiting out my final days, I want you to come and visit me. I want to know who you are and what you've done . . . Think of it as my final bedtime story."

"You have a deal," James said, shaking his hand.

James stood next to the jet, waiting for the Tohmatsu gangsters to arrive. He saw their car in the distance and prepared the pilot for takeoff. Samuel had so far been able to keep track of their friend Troy

Taylor, and James was keen to get to London while they still knew his whereabouts. If they lost him, it could be very difficult to find him before the party.

The black sedan pulled up on the tarmac and the boys exited with big smiles on their face. That was what James liked about these boys—they were always keen to see some action. They didn't just live the gangster lifestyle, they embodied it. They were fucking crazy, but with the discipline of their upbringing, they obeyed orders even in the midst of chaos—and right now that was exactly what James needed.

"Boys," James said with a beaming grin.

Haruto matched his grin. "Thomas, good to see you again, brother. What fucking mess have you gotten yourself into now?" he asked, laughing.

"One you're going to help me clean up," James said, patting him on the back. "Get in"—he motioned toward the stairs—"we're ready to go."

Jiro and Masato followed behind. James had worked with both of them before, in the shoot-out of their disowned brother.

As soon as their baggage was loaded, they were up in the air. James looked over his three companions, who made themselves very comfortable in the private jet.

"All right," James said, taking a seat on the lounge beside Haruto. "You're all on a need-to-know basis for this mission. I'll be taking Haruto to the front line with me, but I intend to keep the two of you out of it as much as possible," he said to Jiro and Masato. The men frowned.

James continued, "However, I don't know what we're walking into, so while that is the plan, the plan might change in a moment." They smiled now.

"We'll be staying at the Tivoli hotel in London. It's a safeguard hotel, and we'll be protected while we're there." He preferred to stay in his safe house, but he was not prepared to expose it to these boys.

"I suggest you get some sleep now while you can. When we arrive in London, we'll check in, and then Haruto and I will do surveillance.

We'll go from there, but have weapons on you at all times, earpieces in, and if you receive any command via that earpiece—either from me, Deacon, or Samuel—I expect it to be obeyed; no questions asked. And, finally, what happens in London stays in London. If I find out otherwise, you'd better start sleeping with your eyes open."

"You have our word," Haruto responded, and James saw a lot of his friend Kyoji in him. With Kyoji no longer second to the helm of the Tohmastu clan, Haruto had stepped up, and he seemed to have adopted the best of Kyoji's attributes.

"Thank you. Get some sleep," James said. He retrieved some pillows and blankets and threw them to the boys. When he looked over his shoulder five minutes later they were all reclined with their eyes closed.

James closed his own eyes, knowing he too would need his sleep. Tomorrow he could find himself in hell.

"Four rooms, please," James said to the man behind the reservation desk at the Tivoli Hotel. It had been a long time since he'd been here, but from the look in the man's eye, James's face had not been forgotten.

"Of course, sir," he said. A moment later he slid four black cards to James.

Every Tivoli Hotel in the world had the same system in place and the same rules.

The Tohmatsu boys joked around as they made their way to their rooms, but James didn't join in. His mind was focused.

James passed each of the men a key. "Meet me in this room in two minutes."

They nodded in agreement and dispersed to deposit their bags.

James closed the door of his suite behind him, washed his face, and dialed Samuel's number.

"We're at the Tivoli," James said. "I'm assuming we still have eyes on our friend."

"Correct," Samuel replied. "But before we get into that, I have a new lead on the CIA plant."

"Go ahead," James said, hungry for Samuel's revelation.

"A series of sequences were reported on her file. Some sequences are a few digits long, others are much longer. Some are purely numerical, some contain letters. I'm running it through some software at the moment, but—"

"They're geographical locations," James said, cutting him off. He'd used that reporting method before. "They're the locations she's been to recently. It won't help us find her, she'll be long gone from any of those places, but it might prove useful to know where she was, and potentially what she was looking at."

"I'll keep working on it," Samuel said. "Now, back to our friend. He's made a few interesting movements today. Picked up some weaponry, made a visit to the Highgate Cemetery—"

"What was he doing there?" James asked, opening the door for his guests.

"I don't know," Samuel said. "He was there for thirty minutes, but I couldn't see what he was up to. It'll help with you on the ground there, I can only see so much on surveillance footage."

"I know," James said. "What else did he do?"

"Stopped to eat a few times, made several phone calls, walked around the city seemingly aimless—although I'm sure that wasn't the case."

James agreed. He was likely supposed to be seen at certain time points, at designated times—it was a non-verbal method of checking in. A method James didn't like, because it indicated two things: he had company, and they were being extremely careful. "Where is he now?"

"At an Italian restaurant. I'll send you details. Be very careful, James, I don't like this at all."

"I will," James said. He didn't like it either.

James looked at the restaurant's location and was pleased to see it was in a populated dining area. "Let's go eat," James said.

22

MAK ASHWOOD

Mak opened the box she had been avoiding for the past few days—photos of her life with Eric. She knew he'd lied about his work, but had their entire relationship been a lie? Had he ever cared for her? Or had he only been using her for something?

She thought it unlikely he'd been using her, because she couldn't imagine what Eric would've had to gain by being with her. She didn't have family money—all she'd had was a promising career, but that was probably evident only to her. Mak doubted Eric would've thought her career would progress as it had, nor as fast as it had.

Mak held the stack of photos in her hand—staring at the lie of a smiling couple in San Francisco.

She shuffled a few more photos through her fingers, looking over each one. Had he tried to tell her about his secret life but she hadn't listened? Had he given her clues along the way? She looked at each photo carefully, trying to remember the circumstances when it was taken.

A knock on the door barely roused her interest. She assumed it was Cami, but it was Deacon who walked in.

"Do you know what time it is?" Deacon asked.

"No, should I?" Mak asked, her eyes lingering on the photo on top of the stack. Mak and Eric had been out with one of Eric's colleagues at a bar in New York.

Deacon sat down in the chair next to her, his eyes landing on the photo. He looked at her, studying her face.

"I know this can't be easy for you," he said. "One of the worst parts of our job is that we sometimes find out information like this, and then we have to deliver it, and it often hurts and upsets people."

There was a tenderness in his eyes, eyes that conveyed far more emotion than his brother's.

Mak sighed. "I just keep wondering how much of his life was a lie. Like these two, they apparently worked together. They were good friends from what I remember. In fact, I ran into this guy just a few months ago, and he was telling me how often he still thought of Eric and how much he misses him. So, did Eric lie to his friends as well as me? I suppose so, right?"

"I don't think your entire life with him was a lie, Mak. None of us do. Yes, his career and what he was doing when he wasn't with you was a lie, but we all think the relationship was real. I think he lied to you to protect you—he didn't want you involved, and with good reason."

"What about this code? You thought he must've told someone he gave it to me. Why would he do that?"

"We don't know. By giving you a code, or at least telling someone he had, the person who needed that code wouldn't immediately kill you. It does, however, mean they could try and kidnap you and torture it out of you. Which is what we think is happening now with Biskup's guys. If Eric thought your life had been in immediate danger, this might've been a last resort to save you, albeit with consequences."

Mak had been digging through her memories like a madwoman searching for gold, but there was no memory of a code. "He didn't give it to me. I don't remember him saying anything about a code."

"The code could be anything, though, that's the problem. It could be a name, a numerical combination, a location . . . At this stage, the code itself isn't important, because we have no idea what it's for. More important is for you to think about Eric's behavior—places he told you he was traveling to, colleagues' names, phone calls he took late at night or in the early hours of the morning . . . anything you thought he tried to hide from you. I know it was a long time ago, but we need you to try and remember."

Mak sighed, not confident in her ability to recall. "Can't Samuel find that kind of information—travel tickets, reservations . . . that kind of thing?"

"Normally, yes," Deacon said, pursing his lips. "But Eric was a little more careful than that. He exited the country on his American passport and disappeared. He had to have assumed an alias and entered whichever country he landed in on another passport."

Mak frowned. "But if he left on his passport, you know what flight he was on, right? You know where he landed."

"Correct, but one flight doesn't tell us enough. We know his early stops were at various destinations in Europe, but from there he could've gone anywhere. He was a smart guy, Mak, so he almost certainly wasn't doing business in the location his flight landed."

"What do you think he was doing?" Mak wondered if Deacon would even answer the question.

"I don't know. Maybe, given that he designed a piece of software that he legitimately sold, it is something along those lines. But, I dare say whatever it was, it was a bit more unique than real-estate software."

"That's a very vague answer, Deacon."

"Because you're asking me a question I have no answer to," he said, crossing his arms over his chest.

"Tell me more about this Biskup," Mak said. "If you know he's the one after me, why don't you try and find him?"

Deacon took a second too long to answer. "We know where he is, Mak. He's not hiding, and he doesn't need to because he's a very powerful man with a virtually impassible security team. Going directly to Biskup would be sending James and me to our deathbeds. We have to find a workaround for Biskup, because he is not an option."

"So how does this end, then?" Mak asked apprehensively.

"It ends when Biskup no longer has an interest in you—when he thinks you don't have the code, or when the need for the code is eliminated. And until we come up with that solution, we're going to protect you, and you're going to learn to protect yourself, hence the reason for my visit." He wiggled his eyebrows, and Mak knew a training session of some form was in her immediate future.

Mak groaned but put the photos back in the box. She'd promised James she would train, and she was going to. If a guy like Biskup was after her, being able to protect herself wouldn't be a bad thing.

"Where's Cami?" Mak asked.

"Busy, so I'm training you. We'll go to the gym for a run and then to the shooting range."

"I really don't like running," Mak said, much preferring her barre classes.

Deacon chuckled. "That's very unfortunate, because given your size the best way you're going to be able to get yourself out of a sticky situation is to run like hell. Like it or not, we're going to make a runner out of you."

"Excellent," Mak said, walking to the bedroom to change into her gym gear.

It was nearing midnight when Mak returned to her apartment. Deacon had made her alternate between sprinting and resting intervals for an hour, and then delivered on his word to take her to the shooting range. Time passed quickly, but Mak didn't miss that he'd extended the weapons session by an additional thirty minutes.

She stripped off her sweaty clothes and turned on the shower just as her phone rang. *James Thomas.*

"Hey," Mak said, turning the shower off.

"Hi. You sound awake, I thought you might be in bed," James said.

"Oh no, your brother decided to make me run for an hour, and then shoot guns for ninety minutes. That wasn't the deal, Thomas. Sixty minutes in weapons training—that was the deal."

James chuckled and Mak grinned at the sound of his laugh.

"I need to call my brother and thank him," James said. "If you think he'll go easy on you, Mak, you've very wrong. Of the three of us, Deacon will probably be your toughest trainer."

"Great. When are you coming home?" Mak joked.

"I'm not going to be much easier on you, so my coming home will achieve little for you," James said. "How are you? How was the rest of your day?"

"It's been fine, really. Much of the same . . . it feels a bit like Groundhog Day. I want my life back—I want to be able to go out and see my friends and family."

"I know," James said. "And you will be able to—this is not forever. It's only for right now, and you need to be patient. Your safety comes before anything else."

"Hang on," Mak said, putting the phone down to wrap a towel around her. She was suddenly cold. "Okay, I'm back."

"What are you doing?"

"I was just getting into the shower when you called, so—"

"Are you naked?" James interrupted.

"I was," Mak said, teasing him. "But now I'm cloaked in one of your massive bath towels."

James groaned. "If I had more time I'd take this conversation in a very dirty direction."

Mak grinned. "That's a shame, I would've enjoyed it."

"Good to know," James said, his voice lower than it had been a few moments ago. "On that note, I do need to go. I can't concentrate when my mind is thinking of your naked body, and I have an appointment in a few minutes."

"James," Mak said quickly before he hung up. "Do you think Eric gave me the code, without me realizing it?"

"I don't know, Mak. I hope he didn't," James said.

23

JAMES THOMAS

I really hope he didn't. He turned his attention back to the current situation. He double-checked his pistol, packed his favorite mutilation utensils and put his earpiece in, checking in with Samuel and Deacon.

"Copy," they said in unison.

"Interesting development tonight," Deacon said. *"That guy—Samuel is sending you a photograph now—we identified in a lot of photos with Eric, the one who was killed in a car crash six years after Eric went missing ... Well, Mak ran into him a few months ago."*

James stilled. "What?"

"Yeah. She ran into him on the street. The guy told her how much he still thinks of Eric and misses him. Apparently they worked together—we know they didn't, but Mak had been led to understand they did."

That's how he's doing it. "He's the one watching Mak," James said. "Eric trusts him, and I bet he's the one who placed the ring as well ... with some help. Samuel—run every surveillance test you can. We have to find this guy, because I think he's reporting back to Eric."

"We don't know for sure that Eric is alive," Samuel said.

They didn't, but James didn't believe he was dead. "Until I have his body, I'm assuming he's alive. This apparently started when the rumors surfaced about his death. Mak's been the target since then. We're protecting her, Biskup's guys are targeting her, but someone else is in this game. And no one else—that we know of at this stage—has a reason to have an interest in her except Eric."

"Or whoever Eric was working for," Deacon said. *"If he changed his mind about this deal with Biskup and decided to sell it to someone else, they definitely have an interest in her. Or even a partner, if Eric had one—if someone on his team knew what he was working on, they might decide to finish the deal. There are a lot of possibilities you're not considering."*

They were all valid explanations, but for some reason James couldn't shake the feeling that Eric was behind the notes, and the ring—the message was too personal.

"Let's not get ahead of ourselves," James said, going back to the new lead. "Let's do everything we can to find this guy, because he's our best chance at getting a few answers, until we track down the CIA plant." James was thoughtful for a moment. "Are we assuming Mak lost contact with him after Eric's disappearance? Is that why she never heard about his death?"

"Yeah, Samuel and I talked about that," Deacon said. *"It was six years later, and he was a work colleague of Eric's. We think it's safe to assume they fell out of contact."*

"Okay. Samuel, where is our friend in London now?"

"I'm sending his location to your phone now."

"Thanks," James said. "We're heading out now."

Haruto and the boys knocked on James's door and he was greeted with eager smiles.

"Let's go," James said.

~

The past twenty-four hours had made the Tohmatsu boys restless. All surveillance and no action was apparently not what they had signed up for. But it was all part of the game, and James doubted it would stay quiet much longer.

James walked with Haruto, while Jiro and Masato walked strategically behind them. As promised, they had thus far obeyed every order and not once strayed from James's instructions. They had been easy to deal with, unlike Kyoji Tohmatsu.

"What's on the itinerary for today?" Haruto asked, puffing on a cigarette.

James was looking at his phone, watching the blue dot move on the GPS.

"That, Haruto, is anyone's guess, and all depends on our friend, Mr. Taylor. Pull up," James said, standing against the wall. Their target was across the road now, purchasing a newspaper by the looks of things.

"Is this the kind of work you do every day?" Haruto asked, casually looking up and down the street.

"Depends," James said. "These days I spend more time in the office creating the strategic plans for our clients. But it's always good to get back out in the field."

"You miss it, don't you?" Haruto asked.

"What makes you think that?"

Haruto stubbed out his cigarette. "Because you're different, you always have been. You've spent too much time in this world to ever leave it behind. You miss the thrill, the bullets, the chase. When you've lived a life fueled by adrenaline, it's hard to walk away."

Haruto was a quietly perceptive guy. James did miss it—he missed his life in the agency—but only one part of him did. The other part loved the life he'd built. He had a good balance now, and it gave him a relatively stable life with just enough action to satisfy the itch— excluding the past month.

"How is the gang without Kyoji?" James asked.

"Different. We lost our brother via the ultimate form of betrayal. But in some ways it's made us stronger, and definitely much more vigilant. People have to answer for their whereabouts and every deal they're making. Everyone is being held account- able for their daily activities—something that should've been in place before but wasn't. We relied too much on trust and the loyalty of family blood. And look where that got us." There was a bitterness in Haruto's voice that James thought would never dissipate.

"Greed and power do terrible things to weak people," James said. His eyes flickered back to the GPS. "I think our friend is heading back to the cemetery."

Haruto didn't look pleased with this development.

"How is Jayce doing?" Haruto asked. "I didn't get to see him last time he was in Tokyo."

"He's okay. His life will never be the same, but he has a great one now. While Kyoji kept him away from the underground world, he did encourage some of Jayce's not-so-impressive behaviors. Jayce seems a lot more settled now, and less impulsive, but I honestly don't see him much because his bodyguard deals with his day-to-day security."

"Kyoji was always so protective of him. They had a good connection, and it showed us that blood doesn't run thicker than water."

"They shared a very special bond," James said. It was an understatement, but he left it at that.

James's assumption of the location was soon confirmed as they walked through a side entry of the cemetery.

"This should be very interesting," Haruto whispered, his head moving in an arc as he took in their surroundings.

"Keep your pistol close," James warned. "Jiro, Masato—hold back another ten paces."

"*Copy.*"

The cemetery was spectacularly eerie. Large, looming tombs were blanketed in lush green surroundings; moss and vines wound themselves around the aged architecture.

"This place gives me the creeps," Haruto said with a shudder.

James looked at the storm clouds in the sky. He didn't want to mention it, but they were running out of daylight, and if Haruto thought the cemetery was creepy now, he was in for a real surprise. James had spent an entire night in a cemetery once and he'd never forgotten the sounds he'd heard nor the things he swore he'd seen.

They walked farther into the graveyard where the greenery seemed to envelop them. James could only see the head of their companion through the headstones, and he appeared to be slowing his pace.

James did a surveillance check, looking for possible hiding spots and exit points. He gently pushed on the door of an old tomb to gauge its resistance. He would be able to open it, but not without making a racket.

Haruto's eyes went wide. "I am not going in there."

James bit his lip, holding back the laughter. "Relax," he whispered, "neither of us are going in there. This way." James tilted his head in his intended direction. They moved to the right of the headstone their friend had stopped at. James crouched low, keeping his head out of sight, thankful for the tall monuments. They veered off the path and crept over the mossy graves. "Be careful you don't slip," James whispered.

When James had a clear view between the headstones they stopped. Looking through his custom binoculars, which fed the surveillance back to Samuel, he watched Mr. Taylor. His lips moved, but James couldn't see who he was talking to.

"I'm going closer. Stay here; keep your pistol aimed," James said.

He kept low, almost crawling, as he silently inched forward. Looking through the binoculars again, he could now see the two men.

"Zoom in on both faces and the headstone," Samuel said.

James adjusted the binoculars, focusing on each man in turn, and then the headstone.

"Running it now. I'll see if there's anything unusual about the deceased, but they probably meet there because they know it's off the surveillance grid."

"Copy," James said as he started moving again.

He needed to hear the conversation—the more information they had the better prepared they would be for the party tonight.

James's eyes landed on a dilapidated cross on a large headstone six rows forward. It was big enough to shield him, and hopefully close enough to the two men to hear them. He needed to move fast,

before the conversation was over, but he also needed to be careful—
the graves were wet and as slippery as ice.

At the fourth row their voices became audible but James kept
moving—he wanted to be able to hear every world.

"Tonight at midnight. I will be there to personally ensure everything runs smoothly."

"We cannot afford a single mistake. How many vials will you be
shipping?"

"Six thousand. The boys have been very busy."

"That's impressive. The new recruits are very efficient. When can
Christos expect the shipment?"

"In three days."

"Excellent—I will let him know. I'll be here tomorrow evening to
collect the case."

"Of course."

"May God be with you."

"And you."

The men shook hands, and James pressed his back against the
monument. He listened to their footsteps, monitoring their movements. James had two men moving apart and had to make a decision.

"No one move," James said in a hushed voice.

"Copy."

James had a team of four, so he could technically follow both of
the targets from the cemetery but the Tohmatsu boys weren't trained
in surveillance. And without James to lead them, he would risk the
Tohmatsu boys being identified, which would cause two problems:
first, the men would know they had been seen and could change their
plans, and second, the Tohmatsu boys could end up dead.

James made a decision: they would continue to follow Taylor,
who would lead them to the shipment.

James stayed in position, adjusting his weight silently and subtly
every now and then to avoid his muscles stiffening.

He peered over the monument again, watching the back of the
second man. He was walking farther into the overgrowth, so James
knew there must be an exit back there.

When the path was clear, James made his way back to Haruto and motioned for him to follow along.

"We need to get a tracking device on our friend," James said. "I don't know what surveillance footage we'll have tonight, and I don't want to risk losing him."

"And how do you propose we do that?" Haruto whispered.

"We're going to follow him back to his hotel. I'm hoping he stops for dinner. I'm going to send you in to accidentally bump into him. The tracking device will be exactly like the one you're wearing, but you're only going to have a second to get it on him, otherwise he'll realize."

"Got it. I'm happy to do anything as long as we get the fuck out of here," Haruto said.

James grinned. "Don't get too excited, we might be back tomorrow."

Haruto groaned. "Could you hear them?"

"Yes," James said, and Haruto knew better than to ask any further questions.

Vials . . . Vials of what? Probably a drug of some sort. The Escanta boys had made their money from heroin, so it wasn't unlikely this group was trading it too. James didn't know who the new recruits were, or what they did, but he prayed they were the next layer—and he was one step closer.

James pressed his back flat against the wall and held his cell phone in his hand. He was looking at an interior view of the restaurant. The restaurant was situated on the corner of the block, and James was positioned at the exterior of the side exit. Jiro had a sniper's position on a rooftop directly opposite, armed and ready. And Masato was seated inside the restaurant, awaiting the arrival of his dinner companion. They were all-systems-go, and everything depended on Haruto's ability to install the tracker.

Taylor was already seated, his chair backed into the corner of a restaurant. It was the table James would've chosen had he been having dinner there. It provided security by isolating him from the other patrons, but he was also close enough to the side exit to make a run for it if needed. The problem tonight was James was waiting outside that exit door.

"*Entering,*" Haruto said.

The multiple cameras on Masato's shirt provided a 360-degree view of the restaurant, and James saw Haruto walk in the front door. He was greeted by the hostess, and then shown to Masato's table. They greeted each other in the jovial manner they used every day, and Haruto showed no sign of being nervous—if he was.

Mr. Taylor's eyes flickered to them but then looked again at the newspaper he was reading. Haruto wasn't going to be able to accidentally bump into him until he got up to use the restroom, or until he exited the restaurant. *One chance, Haruto, that's all you're going to get.* James wished he could've done it himself, but he thought it unlikely Taylor didn't know his face.

Droplets of rain hit James's head, and he looked at the black sky. He needed the weather to hold for another hour at least. He wasn't in the mood to get soaked on the street, nor did he want Jiro's line of sight obstructed by heavy rain.

James turned his attention back to the scene inside the restaurant. A waitress delivered Mr. Taylor's main meal. He thanked her as she put the food down in front of him, but his eyes flickered to Haruto and Masato again. Taylor didn't look concerned, but he was watching them—carefully. It wasn't out of character for someone with Taylor's past and background, and the Tohmatsu boys drew attention naturally with their boisterous personalities and bodies covered in ink. James doubted Taylor had spent much time in Asia, and probably wouldn't recognize the tattoo designs as those of the Tohmatsu clan. Even if he did, he surely had no reason to think the boys were there because of him.

Taylor ate slowly, and James reminded the boys to be patient. Taylor had just finished his main course when the rain began to fall harder.

Come on, Taylor.

His dessert arrived, and he ate it in small bites until barely a crumb was left on his plate. Taylor finally held up his hand, signaling for the bill, and stood up.

"Target moving," James said, praying Taylor needed to use the restroom.

His prayers were answered, and when Taylor closed the door behind him James notified Haruto.

"Restroom. Get into position and hold," James said.

"Copy."

James opened the surveillance footage from the camera Masato had installed in the restroom, keeping two views side-by-side on his cell-phone screen. Mr. Taylor was washing his hands, and Haruto was waiting right outside the door.

"Hold," James instructed. "5, 4, 3, 2, 1—"

Haruto stepped straight in front of Taylor as he exited the bathroom, creating a head-on collision. Haruto had the element of surprise but it happened so quickly James couldn't see Haruto's movements. He did see Taylor's hand go straight to his hip and James assumed he was wearing a holster.

"Whoa man. Careful," Haruto said with a chuckle, holding his hands up in surrender. *"You nearly knocked me out."*

Mr. Taylor stepped back, immediately distancing himself. *"Apologies,"* he said with a nod of his head. He stepped aside, letting Haruto enter, his eyes watching him until he entered the stall, and then he exited the bathroom.

"Got it," Samuel said. *"Well done, Haruto!"*

James exhaled in relief. Now things would get very interesting.

24

JAMES THOMAS

The rain fell in sheets, sweeping in from the side, creating a private symphony as it pelted against their windshield.

"Well, this is just lovely," Haruto said as he stuck his neck out in a vain attempt to see through the rain.

"This is perfect," James said. The heavy rain meant security would take less time getting everyone inside. Even with the marquee set up outside the warehouse, the Docoss Hotel was not adequately prepared for such a rainstorm.

They sat in the van, waiting for enough guests to enter so they would be able to blend in with the crowd. Haruto had done a good job of installing the tracker, and James was watching it on his phone. He'd opted not to use a tracker with a microphone, because they were far easier to detect.

"How many are we at?" James asked Jiro, who he had put in charge of counting—or at least giving his best estimate given the weather conditions.

"Four hundred or so." His words were robotic as he stayed focused on the task.

James noted the time: eleven o'clock—an hour until the shipment was due to leave. "Let's make a move," James said.

They ran across the road and straight up to security. "Anthony Carter and three guests." He assumed the casual role of any other attendee while simultaneously hoping he wasn't going to have to put a pistol to the guy's head to gain entry, and then later pay Mr. Roberts a visit at home.

"Go straight through," he said without a hint of wariness.

Mr. Roberts did well.

The walls vibrated and dance music blared so loudly James knew it was going to be difficult to issue commands via the earpiece. However, if his hunch was correct, the real party would probably be downstairs, underground, where it would likely be much quieter.

"Now this is my kind of party," Haruto said as a topless waitress greeted them.

She leaned forward, her lips not an inch from James's ear. "Welcome to Fantasy. A world where there are no rules and no limits."

James grinned—that was the wrong thing to say to someone like him or any of the Tohmatsu boys.

"Thank you," James said as she handed him a drink that would never touch his lips; not taking one would raise suspicion.

James's eyes darted from corner to corner as they weaved their way through the guests. His view was obstructed by flashing lights and industrial columns that naked men and women were cuffed to. James checked his phone, tracking the location of their friend. And unless he was invisible, he should be standing right next to James. James looked at the ceiling again. There could be a rooftop, but his instincts told him their friend wasn't up there. The boys sat down on a couch, blending into the almost-naked party guests. He watched the movements of the room, not letting his eyes be distracted by the kinky activities unfolding right in front of them.

James checked the time again. They were cutting it close, but James hadn't been able to identify an exit other than those clearly marked—and they weren't the doors he was looking for.

James waited patiently, refusing to give in to the desperation threatening to muddle his mind. He did not want to let this opportunity slip through his fingers, nor would he make a move that would get them all killed.

"Thirty minutes." Samuel's voice was barely audible through the earpiece, but even still James could hear the tightness in his voice.

Perhaps Samuel's words were a good-luck token, or perhaps it was just a coincidence, but just as he spoke James saw a man walk to the left wall of the warehouse and push on what looked to be the wall. A door opened, and he slipped inside.

"Haruto, come with me. Boys, watch the door we enter and let us know if anyone comes in behind us. If I give a command to leave, go. Understood?"

They nodded confidently but James saw fear in their eyes as they looked at Haruto. They were worried James might lead him to his death, and James doubted they were going to leave on his command, but that was something he was hoping he wouldn't have to find out. Haruto nodded to them and then followed James.

James used the column as a compass for the door's location. He was going to get one chance to open it and get inside without being seen, and he couldn't afford to push vainly on the wall, hoping it would open. He counted his steps, taking five diagonal steps from the column. He held his breath as he pushed his palm flat on the wall. It opened. Haruto was quick to follow him in, and they drew their weapons.

They took the stairs down one level. The music was quieter there but James thought they still weren't on the correct floor. Dark red drapes lined a long hallway, and James had no idea what could be behind them. He checked his phone, moving cautiously toward the blue dot. When he reached the spot, a gap in the drapes let him see into what appeared to be a private room. Mr. Taylor wasn't there, but it took James a few seconds to peel his eyes from what *was* there. A man and two naked young women were injecting a red liquid into their veins. A liquid that looked a lot like blood.

Vials of blood?

Dasha had mentioned occult practices, and James wondered whether this was one of them.

James turned, heading back to the stairwell.

"That is some fucked-up shit," Haruto said once they were in the stairwell. James agreed.

The stairwell came to an end and James looked at the final door. He slowly pushed down on the handle, easing it open.

There was no music on this floor, but he could hear voices. Several of them. He let the voices guide him through the warehouse with Haruto close behind.

"The final count has been done and all vials are accounted for. If one single vial goes missing in transit, you will be held accountable. And if that happens, I pray for your soul."

"Do not waste your prayers on me. They will not be needed."

"I hope not."

An engine roared to life, and James angled his head to see, but his view was obstructed by a wall. From the sound of the grunting noise, though, it was a truck of some sort. And it was going to leave soon. James was not prepared to let that happen.

He stepped around the corner and two men came into view: Mr. Taylor, and his old friend from the CIA, Kevin Atkinson.

James couldn't believe Atkinson was mixed up in this. He'd known it was no coincidence when the man had walked past him while he'd been eating breakfast, but he never thought he was linked to this.

James's eyes flickered to Haruto, and he gave the slightest nod of his head. The waiting game was over.

James held his pistol with both hands as he walked toward the two men. Kevin was the first to see him, and he blinked like he couldn't believe what he was seeing. He held his arms up in surrender.

"Drop your weapons," James said, gaining the attention of both men.

"Unbelievable," Mr. Taylor said, looking like he'd just seen a ghost. *In some ways he* is *seeing a ghost.*

Haruto walked behind James, and Mr. Taylor's teeth clenched together. "You!"

"Hello again," Haruto said, and James thought he was grinning.

"Find the driver," James instructed Haruto, keeping his pistol aimed.

"You've been out too long, Taylor, and you're getting sloppy. You should've picked up the tracking device under your collar," James said, and Atkinson rolled his eyes in apparent disbelief. "I'm surprised to see you here, Atkinson."

"Likewise, Liam."

"You've changed your line of work," James said.

"Change is always good," Atkinson said.

"Not always," James said.

He noticed Taylor's roaming eyes, but James wasn't sure what he was searching for. "I suggest you keep your eyes on me," James said.

"You won't get away with this, Smith," Mr. Taylor said. "Or should I call you *Joshua*?"

"Well, gossip certainly does run rife in your circle, doesn't it?" James watched the confidence of the man fade.

"I will get away with this," James said. "Underestimating me is always a bad idea, and it will be your biggest mistake. Men like me have no boundaries or limits to what they will and will not do. And that makes me very difficult to dispose of."

A gunshot fired behind James, but he didn't drop his weapon.

"Found him," Haruto's voice came through the earpiece.

James smiled, indicating it was not his man down. Taylor visibly swallowed, and James saw his hand inch toward his sleeve. James shook his head.

James heard a shuffling noise behind him, but he couldn't take his eyes off these men—not even for a second. Haruto arrived beside him, throwing a dead man at his feet.

"Any more?" James asked. When neither of the men responded, James focused on Atkinson. They'd run in the same circles in the agency, and James was counting on his reputation to coerce the man into cooperating.

"Don't make me do this the hard way, Atkinson. You're out of options, and I'm going to kill you, but it can be an easy death. It's your choice," James said.

"We'll tell you nothing," Taylor said, sealing his fate.

James fired a bullet apiece into Taylor's legs and he dropped to the floor. "Restrain him," James ordered Haruto. "You," he said, nodding toward Atkinson, "start talking. How many are upstairs?"

He wet his lips.

"Atkinson," James said. "Last chance."

The man's chest rose and fell in resignation. "Six."

"Where is this truck going?"

"Bulgaria—"

"Shut the fuck up!" Taylor screamed.

"Gag him," James said to Haruto.

"How long do I have until someone notices the shipment hasn't departed?"

"If I call in the departure now, you'll have five hours until it is scheduled to arrive at the next checkpoint. No questions should be asked until then."

James couldn't trust the man, but he also didn't have a better option at this point. "Call it in. Put the call on speaker," James ordered.

Atkinson nodded and dialed the number. "Christos. The departure is secure."

"Good. At what time did it depart?"

"Two minutes ago, sir."

"Excellent. I'll be in touch soon."

The call disconnected.

"Put your phone on the ground and slide it toward me," James asked.

Atkinson kicked the cell phone toward James with his foot.

"Who is Christos?" James had heard the name mentioned at the cemetery, and he knew this was the man he had to find.

Atkinson hesitated and James fired a bullet into the flesh of his right leg, making him let out a strangled cry. It was a mercy shot—if he hesitated again, James would punish him with a shot in the kneecap. "Christos is the leader of Saratani," Atkinson said between gritted teeth.

"How do I find him?"

"I have no idea. I've never personally met him."

"What is in the vials?" James asked, focusing on the immediate situation.

"Half of them are blood, and the other half are drugs—heroin," Atkinson answered.

"What is the blood for?" James asked.

"Vitality," Atkinson said with a lopsided smile that led James to believe he wasn't onboard with the blood-injecting practice.

"Two incoming," Masato's voice alerted them to the imminent arrivals in the staircase.

Haruto stepped forward, waiting to see if the men would venture to this level. When they did, Haruto gunned them down. James knew that was their cue to leave, but they weren't leaving empty-handed.

James looked at where the truck was parked, and at the end of the warehouse was a roller door. He fired a shot into Atkinson's left thigh and his scream echoed as he fell to the floor. "Where does that exit lead?"

"Into the parking garage of the adjacent building," Atkinson said breathlessly.

"Boys, go and get the van. Drive into the parking garage of the building that backs on to this. We'll meet you there," James said, patting down Atkinson, checking him for additional weapons.

"Copy."

"What about these two?" Haruto asked.

"They're coming with us."

~

James drew the clear liquid from the vial, filling the syringe. It was a reversal drug for the sedative he'd given Atkinson and Taylor before heaving them into the van. They were in an underground tunnel James had used previously, and the rain was still bucketing down, providing an additional layer of soundproofing. The two men sat slumped against the wet, grimy bricks. James squatted in front of Atkinson and administered the reversal while Haruto guarded the entrance.

James stood back, watching him patiently as the drug began to take effect. He'd wanted to interrogate them individually, which wasn't possible in the tunnel, so he'd sedated them. When Atkinson started to wake, James gave him a backhand slap.

"Wake up."

Atkinson opened and closed his eyes a few times before they remained open.

He groaned while his eyes focused on James.

"We never knew what happened to you," Atkinson said.

"I didn't die," James said with a grin.

Atkinson tried to sit himself up, but his bound limbs made it impossible. James let him wriggle around, knowing he wasn't going anywhere.

"Is Saratani the group above Escanta?" James asked.

"Yes."

"How many groups above Saratani?"

"Two," Atkinson said. "Well, two that I know of. There could be more."

"Why are they hunting me?"

"I don't know."

James fired that long-awaited shot into his kneecap.

Atkinson squealed in agony. "I don't fucking know!"

"How did you get mixed up in this?"

"I'm not part of Saratani. I'm a consultant to the group," he said through gritted teeth. "I advise them on intelligence methods. They are an old organization but with a few younger leaders, like Christos. They're very interested in upskilling."

James scoffed. "I can imagine. How long have you been advising them?"

"Two years."

"And have they been hunting me all of that time?" James asked.

"Yes." Atkinson coughed, his chest sounding like it was filled with thick mucus. "You're very hard to find." He slumped to the side and flinched as he tried to sit upright again. James knew his bullet wounds were wreaking havoc on his body.

"I don't want to be found," James said. "What's his role?" He gestured toward a still-sleeping Taylor.

"He's a Saratani member. I've known him only a year or so," Atkinson said between labored breaths. "He's the London contact for the new recruits. He gets his orders directly from Christos, but like me, I doubt he's ever met him."

"How many are in Saratani?"

"Fifty, perhaps? I'm not sure . . ."

Atkinson's eyes closed, and James knew he was about to slip into unconsciousness.

James kicked him in the wounded knee. He jolted awake.

"Someone must know how to find Christos," James said.

"Find Gerard Young—he's the head of operations here . . . He might know how to find Christos. Please, I've told you everything I can. End this, Smith, please," the man begged him.

James wasn't satisfied with the level of information he'd extracted, but he also didn't think Atkinson had any more to give. He loaded two bullets into his chest and then drew enough reversal for Mr. Taylor.

He kneeled down to inject it, monitoring the time on his watch. Sunrise was drawing near, and he had big plans for Taylor—plans which required the safety of the night.

When Taylor came to, the first thing he saw was the barrel of James's pistol.

Taylor gasped and pressed back into the wall but there was nowhere for him to go.

"Don't worry, I have no intentions of using this," James said with a creepy grin. "Your death won't be as painless as his." James looked at Atkinson's lifeless body a few feet away, and Taylor's gaze followed his.

Taylor tensed and James saw him rub his palms together,

attempting to loosen the restraints. James laughed, shaking his head. "You're not going anywhere, but you are going to talk."

"I'm not telling you anything," Taylor said, almost spitting on him.

"You will. Once I start playing with my scalpel, you'll start talking. Everyone does," James said. "How do I find Christos?"

"Christos who?" Taylor asked and James rolled his eyes.

While Taylor was still weak from the sedative, James grabbed his throat and held it against the wet bricks. Taylor wheezed in and out, but he was conscious enough to feel what came next. James drew his scalpel, and, starting at the eyebrow, sliced a circle around Taylor's right eye through his thrashing. When James let go of his throat, Taylor howled. James kicked him, telling him to be quiet.

"How do I find Christos?"

He puffed out short, angered breaths but foolishly chose not to answer.

James grabbed his throat once more and sliced around his left eye, the design matching the right. Blood trickled down both his cheeks—it was quite a sight.

Taylor began to sob, sliding in and out of consciousness.

James slapped him and he opened his eyes.

"Just answer the fucking question." James was running out of patience. And time.

"I don't know. He changes his cell phone every few months, and probably his location too." Taylor was squinting, the skin of his eyes no doubt burning from the scalpel wounds.

"Someone must know how to find him," James said, using his thumb and index finger to hold open one of Taylor's eyes. He held the scalpel up so that he could see it.

"Not me, I don't know."

"Who is the man you met at the cemetery earlier this evening?"

Taylor cursed under his breath. "I don't know his name. He's a messenger—I've never been told his name. I'd never met him until a few days ago."

James changed course.

"Why are they hunting me?"

"I don't know," he whispered. He opened his eyes again, and looked straight at James. "He said you have your father's eyes."

James grabbed Taylor's hair, yanking his head up straight. "Who said that?"

"Christos."

"What else did he say?"

Taylor tried to shake his head but James was still holding his hair tight. "He emailed me your picture . . . it was sent to everyone. I commented on your black eyes . . . that's when he said it. He didn't say anything else."

James sat back on his heels, trying to comprehend the new information. Who was his father, and how did they know what he looked like? James shook the thoughts from his head—he didn't have time to think about his long-lost family right now.

He had work to do, and he wasn't nearly finished with his scalpel.

25

MAK ASHWOOD

There was too much white space on the paper, but Mak's mind was blank.

18666, 6849, Chloe, L817, 2TTB . . .

"What are you doing?" Cami asked, startling Mak from her thoughts.

"I'm trying to remember all of the codes we used for our apartment, the small safe we had, et cetera. None of them seemed significant then . . . and none do now, either," Mak said, tapping her pen on her desk.

Cami looked over her shoulder. "Chloe?"

"It was his family's dog's name."

"Makes sense," she muttered. "That's not very many combinations."

Mak shrugged her shoulders. "We always used the same ones. We didn't have anything valuable in the apartment . . . at least I don't think we did," Mak added. She could no longer be sure what was true and what wasn't.

"It is possible he never gave you the code, Mak," Cami said.

"But what if he did?"

"If he did, the probability of you knowing what the code is isn't even worth calculating. The code isn't the important thing here—his actions are, and where he traveled to."

"But I don't know anything about that," Mak said, holding back the frustration. "What would happen to me if Biskup's guys did manage to get to me? They would torture me, wouldn't they? And then they would kill me once I either gave them the code, or they realized I don't know it, right?"

"They're not going to get to you, so I'm not even answering that. I know this is hard, Mak, but all you need to do is focus on your work. If you can help us by giving us any additional information about Eric —that's great. But if we have to find out his movements on our own, we'll do that; it will just take a little longer."

Mak chewed on her lip. "What if you never get the answers?" Mak's mood had been dark these past few days. The monotony of her routine, her makeshift apartment and not a word from James was taking its toll. The tunnel seemed to be going deeper underground, and there was no light at the end of it.

Cami scoffed. "Have you forgotten who is handling your security? I know James can only tell you so much about his past, and even I know so little about him, but before I met him I knew of him. We ran in similar circles, and he had a reputation of respect and fear I'd never seen before. People looked up to him because he'd done things that were thought to be impossible. He'll never tell you any of this because he's modest. But if I had to choose one person in this entire world I wanted by my side, it would be him." Her voice was full of admiration.

"He doesn't want this for you, Mak—none of us do. But given your relationship, well, he has an additional reason to be motivated. He'll figure this out, and we'll help him, but you need to be patient. James and Deacon won't rush things, and they won't make moves until they're ready—that's why they're so successful."

"How did you meet James?" Mak asked.

Cami smiled. "We ran in similar circles," she said, repeating her earlier words.

"And Deacon ran in the same circles as his brother?"

"Similar," she said.

"Speak of the devil," Mak said as Deacon entered her office.

"What's going on?" he asked, pulling up a chair.

"I was just telling Mak all about how I met your brother," Cami said.

A wicked grin formed on Deacon's lips. "That must've been an interesting story."

"I think she left out a few details," Mak said and Deacon laughed.

"So, this family dinner you want to go to . . . We've decided it's okay, but the restaurant has to be changed. I'll rebook it at a location we prefer."

"We go there because it's my dad's favorite restaurant," Mak said.

"I don't think your dad will care when I tell him the new location is ten times safer for his daughter," Deacon said.

"Okay," Mak said, grateful she could break the routine even for a night. She had never looked so forward to a family dinner.

"Are you going to be my date?" Mak asked Cami.

"I certainly will be."

Mak scoffed. "Welcome to the land of crazy, then. You have no idea what you're in for."

Mak had arranged to bring a second date to the family dinner. If she was allowed an outing, she was going to make the most of it. Kayla was sitting next to Maya when Mak arrived. She was fashionably late due to the series of detours the car had taken on its way there. She walked in from a back entrance and surprised her parents.

"Oh, sweetheart, it's so good to see you," her mom said, wrapping her arms around Mak.

Mak gave her father a hug and proceeded to greet every one of her siblings and their partners. Ten hugs later, she was done, finishing with a final hug for Kayla.

Mak sat down beside Kayla, and Cami sat to her left. Cami's

appearance didn't cause as much attention as Mak thought it might've, the advantage of a large family.

"So, how are you really doing?" Kayla asked.

"Mentally, I'm going crazy, but otherwise things seem to be under control," Mak said.

"Is he here?" Kayla looked over her shoulder.

"No, he's not," Mak said, swallowing a large mouthful of wine as she took in her boisterous family. She hadn't realized how much she'd missed them.

"But he is your boyfriend, right? He has to come to family dinners sometime," Kayla said with a grin.

"I've already warned him about this," Mak said. "And I've told him dinner is nothing compared to the Ashwood family vacations."

Kayla laughed and muttered, "Yeah, never again." She'd been on one with Mak, and later told her it had been the most insane and exhausting holidays of her life. *Welcome to the Ashwood family.*

"But, seriously, why isn't he here?" Kayla asked again.

"He's working," Mak said. She should've said it quieter, because Maya overheard.

"James is working? That's a shame, I was hoping he'd pop by," Maya said.

"You've met him?" Kayla asked.

"Yeah, he was at Zahra and Jayce's engagement party. Very easy on the eye . . ." Maya said. "Both the brothers are. I don't know how you concentrate all day, Cami."

Cami smiled. "They're like my brothers, so it's easy."

"Good genetics run in that family," Maya said. "Anyway, how are you, Kayla? I haven't seen you for months."

"I've been good. Just working a lot . . . I have a big case due to wrap up soon. I think I'm in desperate need of a vacation."

"Yes! Come to Spain with us! Mak and I are going in about four weeks or so."

Kayla's face lit up. "Really? That sounds great. What are the dates?"

The conversation flowed on without her as Maya gave Kayla the dates, and they started making plans. Cami looked at her sternly, no doubt wondering why she hadn't yet told Maya she wasn't going on that trip. Mak returned the look—she would deal with it in her own time. She had still been hoping for a miracle—that this security situation would be resolved soon—and she could actually go with James. But, with each passing day, that flame of hope had flickered a little more until it had blown out completely.

Mak went to take another mouthful of her wine but the glass stopped halfway to her lips. Kayla had pushed the sleeves of her sweater up to her elbows and Mak's eyes landed on the gold bracelet on her wrist. She'd seen the bracelet before, she'd seen it hundreds of times, but tonight she couldn't draw her eyes from it. It was a fine gold-chain bracelet with a flat, circular plate. A symbol was engraved on the plate—the same symbol she'd seen on Eric's locket.

An acrid lump formed in Mak's throat and her lungs burned as she struggled to keep her composure. She sipped her wine now, trying to push the lump down, but the wine only seemed to fuel the fire in her chest.

"Excuse me," Mak said to no one in particular. "I need to use the restroom." As per protocol, Cami also excused herself, accompanying Mak. A move that on any other day would've infuriated Mak, but today it fulfilled her motive.

Cami closed the restroom door and kept her palm flat against it. "What is going on?"

Mak leaned against the vanity, letting it support her shaking legs. "Kayla's bracelet. She's worn it for years . . . as long as I can remember. It has a symbol on it, Cami, and I'm sure it's the same symbol that was on that locket of Eric's—the one that had the photo of me in it. I need to see that locket again, I need to know for sure."

Cami pressed a finger to her ear. "Samuel, can you please send the picture of that locket to my phone? Thanks."

"You have a photo of it? Why?" Mak asked.

Cami drew her cell phone from her pocket as it beeped. "We thought it was unusual that it didn't look familiar to you, particularly given you packed those boxes yourself."

Cami passed Mak the phone. It was the same symbol—there was no mistaking it.

"What does this mean? What does this symbol represent?"

"We don't know. Samuel's been looking into it, but so far he hasn't come up with anything. We didn't know before if it was linked to anything, but given your observations tonight, I think we can conclude it does."

Mak felt like she'd been punched in the stomach. "She is one of my best friends! I've known her for years . . . I-I can't believe this. Is she lying to me, too? Is that what's going on?"

"Keep your voice down," Cami said gently. "We don't know what it means yet. But right now, the most important thing is she doesn't realize you've noticed that symbol. If she's up to something, we want to be able to watch her without her knowing. You need to go back out there, and you need to act like everything is normal. You need to have that stonewall façade you do in the courtroom. You can do this; you're good under pressure. And you need to do it now, because in a way, this might be the most important trial of your life."

Mak nodded, taking a deep breath to steel herself. "I want to know, though, if she's lying to me. I want to know the truth regardless of how much it hurts."

"Let's find out if she is first," Cami said.

She didn't agree to tell Mak, but Mak knew it didn't matter, because there was only one person who really called the shots at Thomas Security—and it wasn't Cami.

26

JAMES THOMAS

His aching body stretched out on the bed, yearning for sleep. It had been days since he'd closed his eyes, and in a few minutes he'd be back on his feet again, making his way once more to the cemetery. And who, or what, waited for him there was the ultimate mystery.

James closed his eyes as he dialed Mak's number. She was at Thomas Security, safe in the apartment in his building, and that eased his mind. He didn't like the latest development involving Kayla, but at least they had another development and, therefore, another lead to chase down.

"Hi," Mak said.

"Hey. How are you doing? Deacon said you did really well at the dinner."

"You know about Kayla, then?"

Even through the distant line, it sounded like she was speaking through clenched teeth.

"I know as much as you know. They're following her now, and we've tapped all of her communications. Samuel and the team are monitoring her very closely, and they'll keep me updated."

"I want to know, James—I want to know what is going on. You can protect me—security-wise—but do not protect me from this. If she's been lying to me, I want to know."

James rubbed his eyes, pausing for a second too long.

"I want to know, James, I need to know—"

"Mak, slow down," James said. "I will tell you, but only when I know the information we have is correct. I'm not going to tell you things that would hurt you and might not be true. I won't do that." James honestly didn't know the extent of Kayla's involvement yet, but he wasn't expecting good news.

"Do you promise you'll tell me as soon as you do know?" Mak asked.

James paused.

"James?"

"Yes, Mak. I will tell you—but not before I'm absolutely certain."

Mak exhaled a shaky breath, and he wondered if it was primarily anger or sadness at the most recent revelations.

"I just . . . I thought once the trial was over everything would settle down. But it's not—it's getting worse. This security case is not what I thought it was going to be."

"It rarely ever is, Mak. I wish I was there with you, but I can't be right now," James said. *Because I'm fighting my past for my future. Because I'm fighting for us, so we can have a life together, and you won't end up in the hands of a Saratani man. Or worse.*

"I wish you were here, too. Do you know when you're coming home?"

"Not yet, but very soon, hopefully," James said.

"Are you often away this much?" Mak asked.

"No, not unless a case erupts and I have to be. I prefer to be in the office overseeing the company. And now, particularly, I want to be in New York because of you. Once this case settles, I'm hoping I won't need to be away much at all."

"Hope is a very dangerous thing," Mak said, speaking aloud the words he'd often thought.

"True," James said. "But sometimes we need to hang on to hope."

Sometimes it's all we have. "You're going to be okay, Mak. Your life is going to change, we know that, and you are probably going to learn a lot more than you want to know. But at the end of this you're going to be fine. And this is only one part of your life. You have a great family and a great career. That is what you need to focus on to get you through this."

James answered the knock at his door. He mouthed *one minute* to Haruto, and closed the door again.

"Mak, I'm sorry, but I have to go. I have a meeting in about thirty seconds."

"Okay," she said.

"I miss you, Mak, and I'm coming home as soon as I can." He hoped he would be leaving in the early hours of the morning, but he didn't want to say that when his plans could easily change.

"I miss you, too. Come home, James," Mak said. "Safely."

"I will," he said before hanging up. It wasn't a promise, but it was a vow he had every intention of keeping.

James opened the door again.

"It's been a long time since anyone shut a door in my face," Haruto said.

James imagined it was. "You'll survive. Ready?"

"Back to the land of creepy," Haruto said with a shudder.

James smiled. "Don't be such a baby."

James watched from behind a crumbling headstone. He was alert, his eyes darting from left to right, his heart rate steady despite the pressure. Christos would know by now that the shipment never left the warehouse—he would've known hours ago—and thus he knew that Saratani had been penetrated.

Once James had been convinced Taylor had nothing else to offer, he'd given him some special attention. James had gouged out his eyes, chopped off his hands and nailed a note to his throat. They'd then dumped his body in a passageway not far from the warehouse. It was James's version of avenging Dasha, and it was the perfect way to respond to their message.

James held his breath as the cloaked man appeared from the overgrowth, walking toward him. He wasn't sure if the man would show—James wouldn't have, given the events of last night—but he couldn't rule out there being a reason for the meeting to continue as per schedule. It was a risk to be here, but with this man being their only potential lead, James deemed it worth the risk.

The man stopped at the same headstone he'd visited yesterday. His shoulders were sitting low and his head was tilted up at the thick mass of clouds above them. *He doesn't look stressed.* That was good because it likely indicated they weren't expecting company. Nonetheless, James wasn't lowering his weapon.

"Incoming. Two targets," Jiro's voice came through James's earpiece.

Jiro was lying in the overgrown grass of a grave about three hundred feet away. Of all of them James had the least concealed hiding spot, but he needed to be closest to the men. He wanted to overhear their conversation before he started firing bullets.

"Hold," James whispered.

James saw the two men enter his peripheral, and he pressed his back flat against the headstone, praying he was not going to become the cemetery's next resident.

The three targets assembled together and one of them handed a briefcase to the cloaked man.

"Have you discovered how Liam Smith knew about the shipment?"

"No, we haven't. We have, however, been able to ascertain how he entered the warehouse . . ."

"And how was that?"

The two men looked at each other, and then back at the man who was obviously much more senior.

"He walked through the front door, accompanied by three other men. We have very few details."

"He walked through the front door?" the cloaked man repeated, shaking his head. "Unbelievable. We don't know how far he's been able to penetrate Saratani, so you'll need to be on full alert. Mr. Smith's warning message was very clear, so stay underground until we learn how he found out about that shipment. I will ensure this is delivered to Christos."

"Understood. We will wait for your next instruction."

"Very good. We're done here," the cloaked man said, tipping his hat toward them.

"Targets departing," James said, his eyes on the cloaked man, retreating into the overgrowth.

"Pass," Haruto said, confirming the men had passed his hideout as they walked the winding paths of the cemetery back toward the front entrance where Jiro and Masato were waiting to greet them.

With enough distance between the three targets, James crawled through the graveyard in the direction of the cloaked man. The man was walking slowly, no doubt due to the slippery moss overgrowth. That worked in James's favor, but he still needed to make up time. James stood, and was gaining on him when the sound of a gunshot echoed through the air.

James lunged behind a headstone but from the corner of his eye saw the cloaked man turn. More bullets fired but this time they were coming in James's direction. The headstone was chipping under the bullet fire, hitting James in the face as he tried to look over his shoulder. He felt another stone chip graze his cheek and he knew he had to move before his shelter completely crumbled.

"Two down," Jiro said.

"Stick to the plan," James said, rapidly scanning his surroundings.

James jumped as another bullet barely missed his shoulder. He had to move, and he had to do it now.

"Haruto, now," James said, and two shots were fired, creating a diversion.

James scrambled across three graves, taking cover behind a larger headstone. He peered around it and opened fire, landing a bullet in the cloaked man's thigh.

James heard a yelp followed by a thud, and he knew the man was down. *Probably not for long.* James sprang to his feet and ran toward the man, shielding his body as he weaved through the headstones.

The man was leaning on his side, firing shots in James's direction, but with a body riddled with pain his reaction time was too slow. James fired a shot as he ran forward, aiming for and hitting the man's pistol.

The man screeched as the pistol was ripped out of his hand. James sprinted forward, praying he didn't slip.

The cloaked man's hand reached into his jacket pocket, and James ducked behind another headstone. He was expecting him to pull out another pistol but when a shot wasn't immediately fired in his direction, James peered over and saw his hand feed something into his mouth.

"No!" James said, lunging for the man. He clawed open the man's mouth but it was too late. "You fucking son of a bitch!" James said, slamming his fist on the man's chest as the pill took full effect.

"Three down," James said through grating teeth. *"Haruto, bring me a syringe."*

James took a deep breath, regaining his composure. He drew his phone from his pocket and photographed the dead man in front of him.

The dead man whom James thought had been the connection to Christos.

Haruto kneeled beside him.

"Cyanide," James said, taking the syringe from Haruto's hand. James pulled a small, thin rope from his pocket and used it as a tourniquet. He drew a full syringe of blood.

Haruto fished out a vacutainer from his bag, into which James transferred the blood.

"We've got to get this back to the hotel and then get out of here," James said.

"I agree," Deacon's voice came through the earpiece.

James opened the briefcase at the man's side. A thick layer of protective foam enveloped a hard drive of some sort. James zipped up the briefcase and handed it to Haruto.

"Let's go," James said, dragging the cloaked man by the arms.

They stopped at an old gate that had seized shut, but it barely came to James's hips and was easy to scale. He dropped the man to the ground and jumped over the gate and into another labyrinth of graves. Jiro and Masato were having a cigarette as two men lay crumpled at their feet.

"We need to move them," James said, leading them to an old tomb with the cloaked man dragging behind him. James fired a shot at the lock and then kicked open the door—it gave a loud shriek in protest. The hairs on his throat stood up as he breathed in the rancid air. He dragged his dead man in and quickly stepped aside so the Tohmatsu boys could drag in the other two. James noted Haruto stayed as close to the door as possible, and when they regrouped outside his face was a shade whiter.

"Samuel, tell the pilot to warm up the engines. We'll pick up our bags, drop off this sample, and be on our way," James said.

"Copy. Francis is on his way to the hotel now to collect the sample, he'll be waiting for you."

"Good, thanks," James said.

James hoped the blood sample would reveal the man's identity. He was a mystery in himself, and the surveillance images from yesterday's cemetery visit hadn't provided a facial recognition match. James didn't know if the blood sample would match anything, either, but it was always a good idea to collect one—he never knew what it could tell him.

The wheels of the jet lifted into the air and James breathed out the tension in his chest. Provided no one shot down the plane, they were out of London—alive. He was going to deliver all three of the Tohmatsu boys back to Haruki unharmed—something he hadn't been sure he was going to be able to do—and he could then get back to New York: to his home, to his family, and to Mak.

He wanted to call her, but he couldn't risk any of the Tohmatsu boys overhearing the conversation. The less they knew about Mak the better, and although they appeared to be sleeping, it was never a good idea to underestimate a gangster. Haruto knew far too much about his life already, but there was little that could be done about that other than kill him—which James wasn't going to do, at least not yet. If he honored his word as Kyoji had, James's secrets were safe for the moment.

James thoughts drifted back to Christos.

Lock your door, Christos. I'm coming for you.

It was the message he'd nailed to the throat of Mr. Taylor.

He wondered how Christos knew he had his father's eyes. It was strange to think that someone knew who his father was. He'd grown so used to being alone, of not having a biological family, he couldn't imagine being a part of one now.

James sighed, closing his eyes. He could think about all of that later, but right now he needed some much-overdue sleep.

James awoke to the ring of his cell phone. "Samuel," he said with a groggy voice.

"I've cracked it. One of the sequences the CIA plant reported links to a laboratory in Istanbul. I hacked their server and you're not going to believe what I found . . . files for Eric. He's dead James, they confirmed it."

Once again Samuel had done the impossible.

"I can't believe it," James said. "Can you verify the DNA match?"

His heart pounded as he waited for Samuel to answer.

"Yes, it appears to be him. The DNA profiling matched a sample from a hospital in New York."

James leaned forward, breathless. He'd been wrong—Eric wasn't watching over her at all. But that meant someone else was watching her, and it was likely they didn't have her best intentions at heart.

"How clean is the match? Is there any chance this result was forged?" James asked.

"Well, without the body it's a bit hard to say, isn't it? The DNA appears to match, but we're assuming the DNA came from the dead body. What if Eric was there that night and the sample came from his arm, for example? The only way to know for sure would be to test it ourselves, and ideally cross-check it with his dental records at least. He had a general practitioner in Manhattan, but they only have electronic files on record for the last twenty years. Deacon is going there and to their storage facility tonight, to see if he can find any paper records. They might've been destroyed, but we might get lucky— some businesses aren't good at managing their documents."

"Good idea," James said. "What did the lab do with his body?"

"I don't know; it's not in the notes."

James knew what he had to do, as ugly as it was going to be. "Hang on," he said to Samuel as he walked to the front of the plane. He opened the cockpit door and said, "Reroute the plane. We're going to Istanbul."

27

JAMES THOMAS

When night fell, James knocked on the door of the closed laboratory. It had been shut for hours, but James had good intel that someone was still inside.

James knocked again, louder and more persistent.

"Can I help you?" A male's voice spoke to him through the intercom.

"Yes. I'm Agent Garcia," James said, holding up his counterfeit identification card. "I'm looking for Dr. Kartal. It's important that I speak with him tonight."

"One moment please."

James noted the time on his watch as he waited patiently. He wanted to do this as discreetly as possible, because the fewer people who knew he was looking for Eric's body the better. He'd brought Haruto with him, but he was waiting at the corner as standby only.

The door opened and a tall man in a white laboratory coat greeted them. He extended his hand. "I'm Dr. Kartal. Could I please see your identification card?"

"Of course," James said, handing it to him.

The doctor inspected it closely, but Samuel only kept friends with the best in the business. Even though it had been a rushed job, James himself couldn't tell it was a fake.

He handed it back to James. "How can I help you, Agent Garcia?"

"I'm investigating the final moments of a body I believe was brought here several months ago. I'm not interested in who brought the body here, as our *intelligence* has already given us that information," James said, watching Dr. Kartal's pupils dilate fractionally. "What I am interested in is the testing that was done, and the samples that were used to match the DNA analysis."

"I think you should come with me," Dr. Kartal said, his eyes flickering to a door to his left and James made the assumption there was someone else in the building.

James followed Dr. Kartal into a private office. Based on the photographs displayed, it was his office.

"Please take a seat," Dr. Kartal said as he sat down in his chair behind the desk.

"I'll stand, if you don't mind," James said, positioning himself where he could see the computer screen.

"I will need the name and the date of birth of the deceased," Dr. Kartal said.

As James said Eric's name, the doctor's hands tensed. He remembered the name, but why?

Dr. Kartal brought up Eric's file and opened the notes section. He appeared to read through them but James's instincts told him he remembered the case very well.

"Yes, this body was delivered to us unidentified. We were provided with DNA records from a hospital in New York. The DNA match was the only testing done—they simply wanted to confirm his identity."

"I see," James said. "They didn't want to know how he died?"

"It was obv—"

Dr. Kartal was nervous, and he fell right into the trap James had laid for him.

"It was obvious?" James asked. "You remember the case, then? Because I can't see anything obvious reported in the notes."

Dr. Kartal looked at the door but he had no hope of reaching it without James getting to him first.

"Dr. Kartal, I have absolutely no intention of hurting you or anyone else in this building. I know the type of men that brought him here, and you were right to do everything they told you to, otherwise they would've killed you," James said, trying to calm him down. "But I need a few answers, and I can't leave here until I have them."

The doctor nodded.

"First, how did he die?"

"The wounds were consistent with an explosion, or blast injury."

"Okay. And the DNA sample that was matched to the hospital records—did you take it directly from the deceased yourself?"

"Yes."

"And the body, what happened to it after you confirmed the DNA match?"

James noticed a slight rash forming on Dr. Kartal's throat. "I didn't know what to do . . . Once I confirmed the match, they told me to get rid of the body and not to speak a word or they would kill me."

"What did you do?" James asked, hiding his impatience.

"I had to tell someone . . . the body was heavy and I couldn't lift it on my own. I called my brother. We wrapped up the body and buried it near a creek we used to play at as children." He shuddered, and James felt a pang of empathy for the man who should never have gotten mixed up in this.

"How deep did you bury him?"

"What?"

"How deep underground did you bury him?" James repeated.

The doctor held a hand to his forehead. "I don't know . . . three feet, maybe? Oh, my."

"I'm sorry I have to do this, but I'm going to need you to show me exactly where you buried him. Can you do that?"

The man looked panicked, and again James tried to reassure him.

"I promise I'm not going to hurt you. You will take me to the site and once I have the body I will drop you off at a gas station with some money to get home. And just like the other men, you will pretend I was never here. That's all I want, and the faster we do this the better."

"Do I have a choice?"

James shook his head. "But you do have a choice between getting hurt tonight or not. Please help me, and I promise you'll never see me again."

The rash on the doctor's neck was flourishing and blotchy, but this unfortunately was part of his destiny. *He must be wondering why he'd been the one rostered on that night.*

"Okay," Dr. Kartal said, standing up.

James called Haruto and instructed him to pick them up at the front entrance. James still hadn't restrained the doctor. He didn't want to scare the poor man any more than he already had. But if the doctor strayed from the plan, he would soon find himself bound and gagged.

James sat in the backseat with the doctor, who gave the directions to Haruto. James had prepared for this event earlier in the day. He'd gone out on his own to get his identification card, and on his way back to the hotel he'd picked up two shovels and some lights and stored them in the trunk.

An hour later, Haruto pulled up at an empty parking lot. It was an isolated location, and James had to admit the doctor had chosen well. Haruto's eyes sparkled with curiosity, but James knew he wasn't going to like what was coming next.

James turned to the doctor. "I don't want to hurt you, but when we get to the location I am going to restrain you because I can't risk you running while we're digging." James caught Haruto's wide eyes in the rearview mirror.

The doctor seemed unable to speak but managed a nod, despite his fear.

James drew his weapon and ordered everyone out of the car. "Haruto, open the trunk."

James grabbed a shovel, keeping his weapon pointed at the doctor. Haruto carried the second shovel and the lights.

"Lead the way, doctor," James said, passing him a torch.

Dr. Kartal exhaled a shaky breath but looked around, as if getting his bearings. "This way," he said, leading them into the forest. James walked directly behind the doctor, and Haruto was close behind him.

They tracked along a narrow, winding path, deep into the forest. The foliage was dense and when a resident bat squeaked out they all jumped.

"Fuck!" Haruto said, his breath fast and ragged. James wished he could've seen Haruto's face. He was walking so close to James now that he could feel Haruto's jacket rubbing against his sweater.

Otherwise, they were silent and James listened carefully, aware wild animals could be a threat, as was the forest itself. He didn't want him or any of his companions to fall or slip down a muddy slope.

Soon James heard the trickle of running water and knew they must be getting close to the creek. The deeper they went, the more impressed James was by the doctor's choice of location. The forest opened to a creek bed, and the doctor turned left, walking for another few minutes. He stopped at a tree with a curved, overhanging branch. He pointed to the ground a few feet in front of him. "He should be there."

James marked the dirt with a shovel, and then bound the shaking doctor. James hung the lights from the tree and tilted his head to the side. "Let's start digging," he said to Haruto.

For a second James thought Haruto was going to refuse, but he muttered a curse and trudged forward, pummeling the shovel into the ground.

"This is stretching our friendship," Haruto said as they began to excavate the creek bed. James grinned.

Over and over their shovels dug deeper. The next time James dug the shovel in it hit something. James knelt down and put his hand into the soil. Plastic sheeting. Bingo.

"We've got him. Let's get him up," James said.

Haruto's shovel flew in and out of the soil, rapidly digging up the earth. They dug the length of an average grave, and then James used his hands to carve out a hole under the body bag until he could lever it up. Haruto gave him a pleading look, but then did the same at the other end. They hauled the body onto the creek bed. James covered his nose and mouth, and then created a small tear in the bag and shone in the light. It was a charred, decaying body. He stepped back, checking his companions. Haruto was watching him with horrified eyes, and the doctor was looking at his hands. James untied his restraints.

"Thank you," James said, looking into the doctor's eyes. "I'm going to need you to carry our equipment, and we'll take the body."

The doctor nodded his head, seeming as eager to get out of there as Haruto.

"Really pushing it," Haruto said as he bent down, lifting the body bag in unison with James.

With the doctor leading the way, weighed down with the extra load, they slowly made their way back through the forest. James was glad Haruto was a fit guy because the dead weight was heavy and the forest presented numerous obstacles. He'd tried to memorize them on his way through, and they avoided most of them, but at one point Haruto slipped and dropped the body bag. James couldn't hold it from one side, and the body dropped to the ground with an eerie thud.

"Oops," Haruto said, pulling his lips to the side.

"Are you okay?" James asked.

"Yes, Haruto said, picking up the body once more. "Let's just get the fuck out of here."

Once more the wheels of the jet lifted in the air, and their plane headed for Tokyo, but on this journey they had one extra guest packed in a casket.

"Please tell me we're going home this time," Haruto said. "It's been fun, Thomas, but I'm about done with graveyards and decaying bodies."

Haruto sat across from James at the table, while Jiro and Masato slept on the couches.

"You know, you're pretty good with a shovel, I was surprised how quickly you dug up that dirt," James said with a grin. Haruto was apparently fine with fresh blood, but once they started rotting he got queasy.

"I just wanted to get the fuck out of there," Haruto said with a laugh that soon faded into a somber groan. "You're in some fucked-up shit, Thomas . . . I hope you can get yourself out of it."

"I'll work it out," James said with a confidence powered by necessity. He didn't have an option other than to work it out—if he didn't, they'd kill him and likely the ones he loved.

Haruto looked into his eyes. "I hope so..." He sounded much less confident than James, but James didn't let that worry him. He'd made a career out of defying the odds, and he was going to do it again.

Haruto sighed, crossing his arms over his chest. "If you get stuck again, call us. I can't guarantee Haruki will give the okay, but if he does, I'll be the first to put my hand up."

"Thank you, I appreciate it," James said.

His original introduction to the Tohmatsu boys had been through Kyoji. James had asked him for a favor, which he'd delivered, but he'd never expected it to result in a long-term allegiance with the Tohmatsu clan. He was grateful for that now, and he wished he could've thanked Kyoji—but like most who died too young, there were too many things left unsaid.

"I can see why you were so close to Kyoji," James said.

Haruto's eyes filled with emotion at the sound of his friend's name. Neither of the men were sons of Haruto's, but they had both become two of the most powerful men in that group.

"Why's that?" Haruto asked.

"Because you share the same values," James said. "You, however, are a hell of a lot easier to deal with."

Haruto chuckled. James had experienced some wild situations with Kyoji, but Haruto would have an overflowing well of them.

"He was a crazy fucker," Haruto said with a wide grin. "He liked you, though, and I think sometimes he did the opposite of what you said just to see if he could get a rise out of you. The boys sometimes call you *Odayakana hito*. It means 'the calm man.' It's true . . . The only time I've ever seen you lose your cool was when that guy took his suicide pill in the graveyard." Haruto gave a laugh. "I thought for a second you were going to start kicking him in frustration."

"I really wanted him alive," James said, chuckling. "I saw his arm going to his mouth, and I couldn't get there fast enough."

"I think all things considering, we did well. I hope you got some of the answers you needed." He yawned and James noted the black circles under his eyes.

"Get some sleep," James said, with every intention of doing the same.

The wheels touched down in New York and James stood up, ready to depart as the pilots finished the taxi. His feet were on the tarmac and he was heading to the hangar as Deacon emerged from the lights.

"Hey, brother," Deacon said, embracing him.

"What are you doing here?" James asked with a wide smile.

"Well, everyone is asleep at Thomas Security, so I thought I'd drive you. And you're going to need a hand with the extra luggage. What a trip, huh?"

"Twists and turns at every corner," James said, putting his bag in the trunk. He was grateful for his brother's company.

"All right, let's get this casket into the hearse," Deacon said.

Deacon motioned for the driver of the hearse to pull up next to the jet. James and Deacon lifted the casket out of the baggage compartment and secured it in the car. They would follow the hearse back to Thomas Security and store Eric's body in their morgue. Forensics would begin testing tonight.

"Any update on the Kayla situation?" James asked as they exited the airport.

"She's done nothing unusual so far, but that doesn't mean anything. I've gone back through the recordings of every communication she's had with Mak. There's nothing unusual there, either, but she does ask about you a lot. Women do talk about these things, but I can't help wonder if she doesn't have an ulterior motive to learning more about you. I definitely think you should hold off meeting her—she's already seen my face, so let's not give her a look at yours as well."

"I agree," James said. "How is Mak doing with all of this?"

"She's all of the things you would expect: sad, confused, and fairly pissed off. She's been dealt a few blows lately, so you can hardly blame her. Her mood might perk up, though, now that you're back."

"We'll see," James said, not responding to the slight change in Deacon's voice as he said those last few words. "I don't know how she's going to react if we confirm this is Eric."

"She thinks he's dead. Still, thinking it and receiving his body are two very different things," Deacon said. "I managed to dig up quite a few additional medical records. There is an old film X-ray of Eric's arm—he broke it when he was about ten—which forensics is going to use as a cross-match. There are also additional paper dental records I was able to get. We have enough sources now to confirm if it's him."

"Good. How's Samuel?" James asked.

"He's tired, and getting a bit short with us. He's under a lot of pressure, so—for many reasons—you coming back to Manhattan and lying low for a little while is a good thing."

Samuel worked tirelessly, and when they needed answers, and needed them fast, they went to him. Sometimes James expected him to work miracles, and sometimes he did.

For the rest of the journey James and Deacon talked over the events of London, and when they finally pulled into the Thomas Security parking garage he felt a soothing feeling of contentment wash over him. He was home, he was safe, and he was back with the ones he loved. He wasn't going to beat Christos and his enemies overnight—it was going to be a long journey—but as long as he had these four people in his life, he would find a way. There was always a way.

"Go upstairs," Deacon said. "I'll take care of the casket and forensics."

"Thanks, Deacon. I appreciate it," James said. He grabbed his bag and headed to his apartment.

He showered, changed into clean clothes, then made his way down to Mak's apartment.

He found her curled up in the middle of the bed. He stripped to his briefs and peeled back the covers. Her body was warm, and her skin felt softer than he remembered.

He pushed the strap of her silk nightgown down her arm and kissed her shoulder. Mak mumbled as she began to wake. James slipped his arm under her waist, drawing her into the crook of his body. He buried his face in her hair and inhaled, letting his chest fill with her scent.

She woke when he kissed the nape of her neck and turned to face him.

"Hey," she said with sleepy blue eyes.

"Hey," he said, smiling. He brought his lips to hers and closed his eyes as he kissed her. She moaned softly and hugged him tight.

"I really missed you," James groaned.

A smile lit up her face. "Good. I really missed you too. Why didn't you tell me you were coming home?"

"I didn't know for sure. I was on my way home once before and had to turn around. But I'm home now, for a little while at least," James said.

Deacon was right: for the next few weeks, he needed to keep a low profile.

"How long is a little while?" Mak asked.

"As long as I can make it," James said, planting another kiss on her lips. His life had taught him many lessons, but the one he was most grateful for was to appreciate the present moment, and he was going to while he could.

"We'll talk more in the morning," James said, his body finally giving away to exhaustion. He hadn't been able to sleep on the plane, and being in a hurry to get back to New York hadn't helped.

"You don't want this . . ." Mak said, pressing her hips into his.

James smiled. "Right now I have everything I want," he said, hoping she understood. "But in the morning, I want plenty of that." He wiggled his eyebrows and she laughed softly. "Can you go into work late?"

"For you . . . yes," she said, tracing his hairline with her finger.

"Thank you," he whispered, unable to keep his eyes open any longer.

28

MAK ASHWOOD

In the morning light, she could see the cut on his cheek and the graze above his eyebrow. *What have you been up to, James Thomas?*

Mak had made a promise to herself from this point forward she would pay extra attention to those around her—she would watch them very carefully. Her career, however unintentional, had honed her ability to read between the lines, and she would fully exploit that skill in her personal life, too. If she had a hunch something wasn't right, she was not going to turn a blind eye and tell herself everything was okay. And this extended to everyone in her life, including the man in her bed. But she had seen nothing, nor felt anything, to contradict his words that he had her best interests at heart.

Mak's stomach rumbled, and it was getting harder to ignore the hunger pains. She wiggled her leg out from between his, but his arms seemed to tighten around her, even in his sleep. She managed to slowly twist her body to reach her cell phone. She'd already messaged her boss once to say she wouldn't be in until the afternoon, but she hadn't counted on sleeping beauty snoozing all morning.

Mak typed another message saying she was still unwell and would be in tomorrow. Two sick days in about as many weeks. *Lucky I won that last trial. Well, won two verdicts.* She hit send.

James stirred, smiling as he opened his eyes.

"Morning," he said with a gruff voice.

"Morning? It's nearly midday," Mak said, laughing at his expression.

"Really?" He lifted his head to look over her shoulder at the alarm clock. "Wow." His head flopped back down on the pillow, and he made no effort to get out of bed. Instead, he secured her legs under his and smirked at her. "You're not going to work."

"Excuse me?" Mak raised her eyebrows.

"Call your boss and tell him you're taking the full day off."

"I can't do that," Mak said with a straight face. "I have a meeting I have to go to. And you can't tell me to call in sick, Thomas."

He rolled on top of her, and she felt his hard cock press against her pelvis. He sucked on her neck, and she moaned despite her best intentions.

"Still want to go to work?"

"Yes," Mak said trying to buck him off. "I don't have a choice, I have to go."

"I think you do have a choice," James said, grinding against her, and Mak felt her nipples harden against his chest.

His lips moved to her beasts, and he licked between them, running his tongue up to her chin. His tongue dipped into her mouth, consuming it.

"Call it in, Mak," he said.

Her body was burning at his touch, and the game only added to her arousal.

"I can't," she said as defiantly as she could, but even she could hear the weakness in her voice.

"I think you're going to call it in any second now," James said, slipping a hand beneath her panties.

She arched into his hand as he teased her.

"You're not playing fair," Mak said.

James smirked. "I never play fair." He bit her nipple and Mak shrieked but the pain quickly melted into pleasure.

"Call it in."

"I already did," Mak said.

James made sure she saw the look in his eyes.

"Yes, Thomas, you won," Mak said, and James chuckled.

"You better make sure this is worth me staying home," Mak said.

"Oh, baby, it'll be worth it," James said, their eyes locking in a heated connection. He rubbed her gently while he restrained her with his body. She tried to touch him, to pleasure him, but he wouldn't let her. Mak had been looking forward to this since James had left, and it didn't take long for the heaviness to pool low in her hips. His powerful gaze was commanding, and Mak wasn't sure she'd have been able to look away if she'd wanted to.

Her legs began to tremble and his fingers slowed—a pattern he repeated relentlessly.

"Please," Mak said, ready to sell her soul for an orgasm.

His eyes flared as she begged him, and this time he didn't slow down. Mak screamed as she dug her nails into his back, curling into him.

"Mak," James said as he brought her mouth to his. He kissed her until her body settled, but he was clearly not prepared to wait—or couldn't wait—too long. He leaned to the side of the bed, retrieved a condom, and rolled it on.

"You came prepared," Mak joked.

"I came ready for you," he said, hovering over her.

He guided his cock in, and Mak gasped as he stretched her. He sucked on her earlobe as he pushed in and out.

"This is going to last about five minutes," he warned her between kisses, "and then I'm going to spend the rest of the afternoon pleasuring every inch of your body."

"Promise?" Mak whispered.

He looked into her eyes. "Promise."

~

James Thomas kept his promise, and as the evening light filtered through the windows they lay cuddled in bed—naked and content.

"Worth taking the day off for?" James asked.

Mak brought her finger to his lips, wiping away his smirk.

James chuckled, and then bit her finger, clamping down.

Mak flinched. "Yes, it was worth taking the day off. It might just be the best afternoon of my life," Mak said.

James beamed a grin. "Really? That pleases me more than you can imagine. And I fully agree. I think we should do this more often."

"Oh, really? Who do you think you're dating? I have an important career that requires me to be at work every day, not lounging around in bed fucking my boyfriend." The word slipped from her mouth and she realized it was the first time she'd said it aloud in front of James. *Boyfriend.* "Does that sound weird to you?"

"I'm glad you think that, because it's very weird for me," James said. "Weird in a good way, though."

"Good to know," Mak said, with a soft laugh.

James scooped her into his arms, curling his body around hers. He nuzzled his face into her neck and moaned softly. "Are you hungry?" James asked.

They'd ordered in food for lunch and had eaten it in bed. Mak couldn't see dinner being much different.

But James apparently did. "Do you want to eat before or after we train?"

"Train?"

James tilted his head up to look at her. "Did you really think you were getting out of your training sessions today?"

Mak grinned—that was exactly what she'd thought.

"Well, I definitely don't need to do any cardio seeing as you've already taken care of that. So maybe we'll just shoot some things."

"Maybe not," James said, pinching her. "Sex is a bonus only. And speaking of shooting things, I hear you've improved dramatically. And you're shooting at the chest, which pleases me," he said.

"I'm sure it does," Mak said, pinching his shoulder. "When do I get my own gun?" Mak didn't want one at all, but she did want to see his reaction.

"When you're a decent shot," James said and Mak smacked his arm.

"You said I've improved dramatically!"

James chuckled. "Improved. That's different from good."

He anticipated her move and grabbed her arm, twisting it behind her. "And that's exactly why you need to learn to shoot," he said, raising one eyebrow.

Mak rolled her eyes. "Are you going to train me tonight?"

"Yes. I have no intention of leaving your side until you go to work in the morning."

Mak smiled. "Okay. Let's train first, because if you're anything like your brother I'll be vomiting if we eat dinner beforehand."

James laughed and Mak noticed his eyes didn't leave her as she got out of bed and dressed in her gym gear. The sheets were draped low on his hips, revealing his rippled abdomen, formed to a V. One arm rested behind his head, and it was a quite sight to behold.

When she was fully dressed, he got up, pulling on a pair of track-suit pants and a T-shirt.

"I don't think I've ever seen you wear anything but jeans," Mak said.

"I wear jeans every day because they're practical," James said.

"Practical how?"

"The brand I like has lots of pockets, which are useful for storing things I might need when I'm out and about," he said.

He had a strange look on his face but Mak didn't know what to make of it.

"What kinds of things?" Mak asked.

"Cell phone, pistol, spare earpiece and other bits and pieces," he said, putting on his T-shirt. "Let's go."

"*Let's go*," Mak said, repeating his favorite phrase.

~

James's back was turned to her as he spoke in a hushed voice. It was the second phone call he'd taken during dinner. Mak stirred her food around on her plate as he stood in his kitchen. It was a conversation she was definitely not supposed to overhear, which only intrigued her more.

"Call me back," James said, walking back to the dining table.

He sat down and started eating like nothing unusual was going on.

"Is everything okay?"

"That depends on the next call," he said, his appetite not appearing to suffer from any stress.

"Are you leaving again?" Mak asked.

"No, it's not that case," he said. "Have you had enough to eat?"

Mak tilted her head. She didn't like the feeling stirring in her stomach.

"Is this about me? If this is about Kayla, I want to know. I deserve to know the truth about what is going on."

"It's not about Kayla," James said.

His cell phone lit up, and he hesitated for a second before answering it. Mak would've missed it except she was watching his body language like a hawk. *What is going on?*

He turned his back, speaking only when she was out of hearing range.

She saw him rub his neck and then inhale deeply. *I'm not wrong. Something isn't right.*

She pushed her plate away, her appetite not as iron clad as his. She strained her ears to hear but doubted he was going to make the mistake of letting her overhear another conversation.

What seemed like an hour later, but was probably only minutes, he turned around. He chewed his bottom lip as he walked back to the dining room, but he didn't sit down in his chair. He sat beside her.

"What's wrong?" Mak asked.

James inhaled deeply and took her hand.

"You said you wanted to know the truth about Eric and what he was up to. I don't have those answers, yet, but I do have some information. You told Deacon you thought he was dead. What made you think that?"

Mak's legs felt heavy and her hands began to tremble. "I don't know . . . I just . . . I knew him—well I thought I knew him—so I couldn't think of any reason why he'd disappear except if something had happened to him. And each day that passed was harder and harder to believe he was coming home. I gave up, I suppose."

James nodded. "He's not coming home, Mak. You were right."

"How do you know for sure?" Mak asked.

"We found a laboratory that had a deceased file attached to his name. We have since carried out our own testing: DNA, dental and bone structure. We have no doubt it is him."

Mak's vision spun, and she leaned on the table for support. For so long she'd wanted a body to bury, but she'd never truly expected she'd get one. And now that she had, she wasn't prepared for it—if you ever could be.

James put his hand on her waist, keeping her upright.

"I . . . I can't believe it. How? Where is this lab?"

"In Istanbul."

Mak felt her chin drop to her knees. "Istanbul? What was he doing there?"

"We don't know," James said.

"Did he die there?" Mak's voice cracked as she said the words aloud.

"It's hard to know for sure, but I think so."

A tear slipped from the corner of her eye. She'd given up thinking Eric would walk through the door, but she'd grown comfortable with not knowing what happened to him. People said it was harder to not know, to not have closure, but not knowing had let her live in comfortable denial without even realizing it.

Mak quickly wiped her cheek and looked away.

"Mak, it's very different to think someone is dead than it is to be told they are. It's okay to be upset." James pulled her chair toward him.

"He's been gone thirteen years . . . I knew he was dead . . . But it's still hard to hear it."

"Of course it is," James said softly, brushing her hair off her wet cheek.

Mak felt more tears in her eyes but they were tears she wanted to shed alone. "I'm going to use the bathroom."

She closed the door behind her and looked at her reflection in the mirror. *A widow.* She was formally a widow. She splashed cold water over her face as she fought back tears. Who was she crying for? The man she had married in her young, innocent twenties? Or a man who had lied to and deceived her? The tears continued to come without any answers.

Her chest heaved and shuddered as she shed her raw emotions. When she finally composed herself, she had no idea how much time had passed. She splashed more water on her face and dabbed her red eyes and blotchy face dry.

She walked into a dark hallway but saw the light on in James's bedroom.

He emerged from the room and leaned against the doorframe.

"What do you want to do tonight? You can stay here, or, if you want to go downstairs and stay in your apartment alone, that's fine and I understand."

Mak shook her head. "Can we just go to sleep?"

He came to her and kissed her forehead. "Yes, we can. Come on," he said, taking her hand.

The television was on in his bedroom and the sound of it comforted Mak. It drowned out the noise in her mind, and she curled up into James's arms, listening to the news and the problems of the world. He stroked her back until she fell asleep.

29

MAK ASHWOOD

Tortured screams jolted Mak from her sleep.

"Shh, it's okay," James said, pulling her to his chest. He put his hands over her ears, but she pushed them away.

"Is that Deacon?" Mak felt a surge of adrenaline as his cries carried through the walls.

"He's okay, he's just having nightmare. It'll be over soon," James said, trying once more to cover her ears as he guided her body back under the covers.

"Nicole! Nicole!"

Mak cringed at the sound of his voice. "Shouldn't you wake him up or something?"

"It only makes it worse."

"Who is Nicole?"

James sighed. "Someone he loved, who died very tragically. Mak, please don't ever bring this up to Deacon. He would be upset if he knew you'd overheard his nightmare."

"Sure, I understand," Mak said. "What did you mean when you said it will be over soon?"

"I've heard it many times before. His nightmares are rare nowadays, but he occasionally still has them. And it seems to always be the same dream. I've tried waking him up before, but he doesn't react well. Deacon is a man who likes to talk a lot, but not about his own feelings. He likes to be alone after something like this, but he'll be okay in the morning."

"How loud is he screaming? It sounds like he's in this room," Mak said, letting James pull the covers over their heads now.

"Our bedrooms back up to each other. There's not a lot of insulation between our rooms, and that's intentional—if someone were to get into his apartment and try to kill him I would want to be able to hear it and help him. We never intended to have women here, so the soundproofing hasn't been an issue, but now I'm wondering if we need to do some minor renovations. Have you noticed we've never had sex in this bedroom? That's not an accident."

"But we've had sex in my bedroom. Does that mean Cami has heard?" Mak felt her cheeks blush in the dark room.

"No. Samuel and Cami's bedrooms back up to each other. The guest apartment is set up differently, and those walls are well insulated. We wouldn't want anyone eavesdropping on our conversations, would we?"

Mak ignored his comment—she wasn't prepared to apologize then, and she wasn't now, either.

Deacon's wailing cries were fading in intensity, but Mak knew whatever he was seeing must be painful. "I feel for him," Mak said.

"I do, too," James said, and she could hear the emotion in his voice. He kissed her forehead and squeezed her tighter. "He'll be okay, though. Don't let Deacon's pretty-boy looks and charming demeanor fool you—he's strong, mentally and physically."

"It obviously runs in the family," Mak said. "Hang on, who is the older brother?"

"I am, by a couple of years," James said.

The room was silent again, but Mak was wide awake. Now that the shock of confirming Eric's death had worn off, Mak had questions. A lot of them.

"Can we talk about Eric?" Mak asked.

James rolled over to turn on the bedside lamp and settled on his pillow, facing her. He nodded, and Mak tried to line up the questions, but there were too many. "What was he doing in Istanbul?"

"We don't know. Some form of business, definitely in the illegal trade. Whether he was based there or was just visiting for some reason, we don't yet know. There is a lot we don't know about him," James said.

"You said you were running your own forensics, so you found his body then, right?" Mak forced out the words.

"Yes, we found him. He was brought to the laboratory late one night, but after his identity was confirmed, the men no longer wanted his body. So the man who conducted the testing stored his body, not sure what else to do with him."

"What forensic testing are you doing? All that must be left are skeletal remains, right?"

He had that sympathetic look in his eyes again. "Not exactly. Forensics are still carrying out testing, but based on results so far, we think he probably died about four months ago."

Mak's body flushed cold. "Months? You mean years, right?"

"Months, Mak. He died recently; I looked at his body; I can confirm that without forensics."

He was alive all this time. And not once did he contact me.

The sadness she'd felt earlier vanished, replaced by a newfound anger.

"Where is he now?"

James sighed. "He's in New York. I arranged to bring him back. He's in a morgue with forensics at the moment, but after that, if you want to bury him you can. If not, we'll take care of him."

Bury him. The day had finally come that she could bury her husband, but now the spiteful bitterness in her heart had stolen all of the peace.

"What should I put on his headstone? *Beloved husband*? Or *lying bastard*?"

James looked at her with a blank face. "Perhaps just his name would be best."

"I don't even know his date of death to put on the headstone," Mak said.

James shrugged his shoulders. "We'll make it up based on what we do know. The details don't matter, Mak—the important thing is that you do what is best for you. There is one thing, though—I don't want you to tell anyone about this yet, not even your parents. Until we know exactly what he was up to, I would prefer no one realize we found his body."

"So, it will be a funeral party of one, then?"

"And your security team," James said. "His family and friends can pay their respects when your case is resolved."

Mak nodded her head. "Thank you, I think."

"I think in years to come you'll be glad you buried him, regardless of how he wronged you." James brought his hand to her face, massaging her clenched jaw.

"I hope so," Mak said. "Do you think if I'd hired you, instead of the other investigator, you would've been able to find him when he first went missing?"

"Yes," James said.

Mak looked into his bottomless eyes. She wondered how many of his secrets she'd eventually find out. "Tell me something about you, something no one else knows."

"That no one else knows? Not even Deacon, Cami, or Samuel?" James asked.

Mak nodded.

He pressed his lips together and his eyes thinned as he thought it through. "Hmm . . ."

He thought about it for so long Mak had almost given up, but when he spoke it was worth the wait.

"My favorite place in the world is Iceland. Have you ever been there?" James asked.

"No."

"It's so beautiful. I spent nearly a month there with a client. He was building a holiday home, and I was designing and installing the security system. This home sits atop a mountain and has the most amazing views of the turquoise hot springs below. It's quite a magical place.

"The client is one of our most loyal—he's been with us from the beginning of Thomas Security. While I was staying with him he offered the house to me, told me I should bring my girlfriend. I laughed, but he grinned and told me it was a lifelong offer . . . I could take him up on that offer anytime. Do you want to go to Iceland with me?"

"Tomorrow?" Mak asked with a grin.

"No, not tomorrow," James said with a chuckle. "But definitely as soon as your security situation settles down a little. It's an extremely secure property, so it could be our first vacation together."

"I would love to go to Iceland with you," Mak said, wrapping her arms around his neck.

"I'm beginning to like this vacation requirement of yours," James said.

"I hope we get to go on a lot of vacations together." Mak watched his face, and it was one of those rare moments when he didn't hide his emotions from her.

"I want that too," James said with a deep voice.

He gave her a kiss full of passion and want.

"Make love to me," Mak said.

He smiled. "You have to be very quiet, though. Silent. Promise?"

"Promise," Mak whispered, looking into a pair of heated black eyes.

Throughout the following days, Mak fought between her oscillating emotions—the betrayal of her husband, and the relief that she had a body to bury. Forensics was due to conclude their testing, and she could prepare his funeral arrangements. She held two catalogues in her hand—one for headstones and one for caskets. All she had to do was choose them, and the rest Thomas Security would take care of. A priest had already been booked, a grave plot purchased, and tomorrow she would bury her husband.

"Should I wear black?" Mak asked Cami.

"Only if you want to," she said.

"I asked James if I should put 'beloved husband' or 'lying bastard' on his headstone."

She pressed her lips together. "What did he say?"

"Mr. Calm said to just put his name."

"Mr. Calm would," Cami said. "You have a right to be angry, Mak. If I were in your situation I'd be steaming from the ears."

"I wish I knew what he'd been involved in," Mak said.

"I think you're better off not knowing," Cami said. "But I do know you have to make a decision on those tonight if we're going to bury him tomorrow," she said, gesturing toward the catalogues.

Mak flicked through the pages once more and settled on a black granite headstone with gold writing. And a black casket with gold hardware. *Tomorrow it will all be over.*

Mak stood at the foot of the grave, her eyes cast down at the black casket that held her husband's remains. As much as she didn't want to shed any tears for him, they came like unwelcome guests. Cami passed her a tissue, and she dabbed the corners of her eyes.

The priest said a prayer for Eric's soul, but Mak wondered if his soul was past redemption. Or if his soul was even still inside his body. Could Eric see her now, standing over his grave, bidding him farewell from this earth?

The longer Mak looked at the grave, though, the less resentment she felt toward him. He'd spun a web of lies around their life together, but Mak couldn't help but feel life had punished him by taking his soul early.

Goodbye, Eric. She put the flowers she'd been holding onto the casket. *I'll see you on the other side one day far from now, and then you can tell me why.*

Mak balled up the wet tissue in her hand, and when Eric's casket was lowered into the ground, she threw it into his grave—burying her tears with him. She let out a shaky exhalation and thanked the priest.

"I'm ready to go," Mak said, taking one last look at her husband's grave.

30

JAMES THOMAS

She looked beautiful in black, but nothing else was beautiful about today. Mak's slight body trembled as she exhaled, her eyes lingering on the casket holding her husband's remains. He would be buried now—again—and James hoped it would give her some closure.

She lifted her eyes and nodded to him.

"Moving," James said, and his security team assembled. Their cars were nearby, greatly minimizing the risk, but he couldn't be too careful. His intentions were to only bury one body today.

James wanted to hold her in his arms and comfort her, but it was an unusual situation, and he couldn't predict how she would react. Sometimes she seemed to need his comfort, and other times she wanted to be alone. He let her make the first move, and when she slipped her hand into his, he felt his body warm. He gave her hand a little squeeze but kept up the pace toward the car.

He did, however, cast his gaze across to his brother, who had been unusually quiet today. James had known the funeral would be hard for Deacon because it was a reminder of something he would never get—he would never be able to bury Nicole's remains. When James had rescued Deacon, he'd only had to take one look at Nicole to realize she was gone. Hauling Deacon's immobile body out had been difficult enough, and if James had tried to take Nicole with them they would've all been killed. James made the decision to leave her body behind, and where her remains were now was a mystery they would never solve.

In the car, Mak sat quietly with her emotions. James's eyes darted from point to point, watching the traffic, and watching for a tail. He could see his brother doing the same. It wasn't just the risk of having Mak in the car today, but they also couldn't reveal their location. James couldn't imagine that Biskup's guys would be pleased to learn that they'd found Eric's body, and James couldn't predict the consequences if they were to find out such news.

What James wanted to test, though, was Kayla's involvement in this situation. He wanted to create a catalyst for her to take action but, unfortunately, his best ideas all involved Mak—and today was not the day to spring that on her.

Deacon pulled up in his designated parking bay and everyone went their separate ways. James took Mak up to his apartment.

"Are my eyes still red?" she asked, rubbing them.

"No," he said, taking her hands away from her eyes before she rubbed them red. "You did well, and you did the right thing by him."

"I feel so tired." She rested her forehead against his chest, and he ran his fingers through her hair.

"Lie down and sleep for a bit," James said, leading her to the couch.

She sank into the large pillows, and he draped a blanket over her.

"Thank you for organizing everything for today. It's ironic, don't you think?"

"Yes, but that doesn't worry me . . . I like being able to take care of you." He was surprised at how much he did enjoy caring for someone. Protecting someone was one thing, but to truly care for someone and make their life a little bit better was a gift, not a burden.

"For a guy who doesn't have girlfriends, you're surprisingly good at it," Mak said, smiling for the first time today.

"You make it very easy," he said, lying down next to her. He watched her eyes close with exhaustion and stayed by her side until she fell asleep. He pulled the blanket up over her shoulders and tiptoed out of his apartment and down to Samuel's office.

Cami pulled out a chair for him.

"What's new?" James asked no one in particular.

"Not much, which is a problem," Deacon said.

"No leads on Christos. I've gotten a bunch of codes from the hard drive that was in the briefcase—but I have no idea what they're for. I haven't gotten an identification match for the cloaked man from the cemetery. And we have nothing else on Kayla. Things are going swimmingly."

Samuel let out a frustrated sigh, and James knew this was getting to him—there was nothing Samuel hated more than unsolved mysteries with dead leads.

"We have to provoke Kayla," Deacon said.

"I agree, and I came up with an idea," James said. "I want Mak to call her. She'll tell her I called and told her I found Eric's body in Mexico, and I'm bringing him home. I don't really want to use his body as the trigger, but it's the most powerful option we have at the moment. If she's as careful as whoever has been watching Mak, she's only going to take action if it's for something big."

"Why Mexico?" Deacon asked. "Because it's way off where we found him?"

"Yeah. And it might serve as a bonus for us if they think we're looking in all the wrong places. But Mexico is a feasible place for someone to end up dead if they went missing from New York," James said.

"The other option is to use you as the trigger, rather than the body. Mak could tell Kayla you're back, and she wants to arrange drinks so you can meet her friends. Of course those drinks will get *postponed*, but it might work," Deacon said.

"I thought about that, but I don't think it's powerful enough. She might just alert whoever she reports back to, but I want this to filter all the way up to whoever is in charge," James said.

Deacon nodded. "Thoughts?" he asked, looking at Samuel and Cami in turn.

"It could work," Samuel said, and Cami shrugged her shoulders noncommittally.

"Let's do it. What's Mak doing now?" Deacon asked, sitting up straight.

"She's asleep," James said, watching the disappointment flood Deacon's face.

His brother chuckled. "That's an anticlimax."

James laughed with him, but he was interrupted by a telephone call. *Apparently not.*

"Hey, Mak," James said, watching his brother's face light up again.

"Where did you sneak off to?" Mak asked.

"I didn't sneak off anywhere . . . I'm working in Samuel's office."

"What are you working on?"

"What am I working on?" James repeated the question for Deacon's amusement, and he saw his brother smile. As much as Deacon didn't like their relationship, James thought he secretly liked that Mak questioned him constantly and wasn't intimidated by him.

James debated whether or not tonight was the appropriate time to ask her to make the call. She'd been exhausted when they'd arrived home, but she seemed more like herself on the phone now. If she were just a client, he'd insist she do it—because the sooner they had another lead the better.

"Actually, we were just discussing Kayla," James said.

"What has she done?" Mak quickly asked.

"Nothing—that's the problem. We want to provoke her to do something out of the ordinary, but that would involve creating a trigger," James said.

"Do it, but I want to know what happens as the result of it." Her voice was strong, and James knew this was not something she was going to back down from.

"We've come up with an idea, but we need you to be involved for it to work."

"What do you need me to do?"

"Call her," James said. "Call her and tell her I found Eric's body in Mexico, and I'm bringing him home so you can bury him."

"What's that going to achieve?"

"We think, based on that matching symbol, they were both part of some organization. They knew Eric, and his body being found would be of interest to not just Kayla but whoever is in charge—we think. It might work, or it might not, but it's worth a try if you're okay with it."

"Sure. I need to know the truth about her. Should I call her now?" Mak asked.

"Yes, might as well. You can call her from your mobile, and Samuel will record it all for us."

James didn't mention that the call would be on loudspeaker in Samuel's office—he didn't want to give her stage fright.

"You need to sound like you're in shock, Mak, you—"

"I know how to sound on the phone," she said gently. "I've just been through the emotions."

"Okay. Call her whenever you're ready. If she starts asking questions, just say Mexico is all I told you and you're waiting until I get back for further details."

"Got it," Mak said, sounding like a woman on a mission.

"I'll come up once it's done," James said before ending the call. He instructed Samuel to load the surveillance views they had for Kayla. The screens flickered and displayed six different views—the angles weren't as good as James would've liked, but Deacon had installed them in a rush, and illegally.

A few seconds later the call played through the speaker system and James saw Kayla in her office. She picked up her phone.

"Hey, Mak. What's happening?"

Mak didn't respond immediately and James thought for a second the plan wasn't going to work. What he didn't realize was how good of an actress his girlfriend was.

When Mak finally spoke, her voice was trembling. *"Kayla, I just got a call from James . . . He found him . . . He found Eric."*

James watched Kayla's reaction, and she truly looked shocked.

"W-What do you mean?" Kayla stammered.

"James found his body, Kayla, in Mexico. I always thought he was dead but now it's real and . . ." Mak's voice cracked and James realized today was the perfect day to do this because Mak was still emotional, and that made the call all the more believable.

"And," Mak continued, *"he's bringing Eric home. After all these years, I can finally bury him."*

"I . . . Mak, I don't know what to say . . . I can't believe it. Mexico doesn't make any sense. Why was Eric there? Where exactly did James find him?"

James and Deacon's eyes met for a second.

"I don't know . . . He said he'll explain everything when he gets home."

"When is that? When will you have Eric's body?"

"Tomorrow, I think, but I'm not sure. The line was bad and he didn't have much time. Anyway, I just wanted to call you first. I don't know if I should start making funeral arrangements or—"

"Mak, maybe just wait until James gets back. How does James know it's definitely him?"

"I don't know," Mak said. *"But I know he wouldn't tell me unless he was certain."*

"Wow," Kayla said, slumping forward on her desk. *"I'm sorry, Mak, I'm sorry you have to go through this. It should never have been like this."*

"No," Mak said, *"it shouldn't have. But it is, so I guess I just have to deal with it . . . Kayla, Cami's just arrived, so I have to go. I'll call you tomorrow."*

"Okay. Call me if you need anything, any time of the day or night," Kayla said.

"Thanks, that means a lot," Mak said, and James thought she was layering on a final layer of guilt.

The call disconnected and James watched Kayla carefully now, because what she did from here would give away her secrets.

She buried her face in her hands and her shoulders shook slightly. Was she crying? Their cameras had audio but James couldn't hear anything, so if she was crying, she was barely making any noise. She then stood up abruptly and closed her office door. She paced the floor, scratching her throat—a stress reaction.

"I can't do this," Kayla said. *"I can't do this anymore."*

"Bingo," Deacon said, leaning toward the screens.

Kayla repeated the words over and over again, working herself into a frenzy. She shook her head and then walked back to her desk, retrieving something from her handbag. A cell phone. A different cell phone than the one Mak had called her on.

She held it to her ear and Samuel's fingers started flying across the keyboard.

"Ben, it's Kayla. I can't do this anymore, I don't want to be involved, I want out." Kayla started rambling and within a few seconds Samuel delivered the bad news—she was using an untraceable phone.

"What happened? Mak just called. She thinks this James guy is bringing home Eric's body. I can't do this, I can't let her bury someone, thinking it's her husband.

"I don't know, Mexico somewhere. He's bringing the body home. This was not the agreement. I was only supposed to watch over her and report back to Eric if she was in danger. It was never supposed to get to this. She can't do this, she can't bury the wrong man.

"No, I haven't forgotten . . . Yes, I know he got me clean, but he's used it against me every day since. I want out; I'm not doing this anymore.

"I do have a choice—

"You don't need to remind me, I know what that crazy bastard is capable of.

"Where? Okay, I'll meet you there."

Kayla hung up, grabbed her handbag and left her office. James had a team following her and advised them she was on the move, and not to lose her.

"This is very interesting," Deacon said.

"Why hasn't it even occurred to her that it might actually be Eric's body? She never considered it, not for a second. She's certain he's alive. Why?" James was not liking the prickly sensation on his skin.

No one in the room had an answer for him.

James watched the surveillance feeding through his team's binoculars. Kayla walked six blocks and then turned into a passageway.

"I've activated the microphone in her cell phone, but if it's in her bag I don't know what feed we'll get," Samuel said.

"Call it and say it's a wrong number. She might keep it in her hand," James said.

It was a long shot, and it rang and rang before she finally answered. But when she did, Samuel played out the plan and they got lucky when her faint voice fed through to the speaker system.

"You need to calm down," a male voice said. *"You can't walk away from this, and neither can I. If either of us causes trouble, he'll kill us both, and you know it. You have to let Mak bury that body if that's what we're told to do."*

"Have you called him?"

"Yes, it went to voicemail."

The entire office was still and silent as they strained to hear the conversation.

"You're freaking out, Kayla, and you need to calm down. You've been lying to Mak this entire time, and this body situation is no different."

"I haven't been lying to her—I even told her in the past not to give up on him. But this is different; it's so different. It was one thing for her to make assumptions about what happened to Eric, but for her to bury him . . . She's talking about funeral arrangements for Christ's sake!"

Another phone rang and James held his breath. *"Hang on . . . Hey. Yes, that's correct. They think they've found your body in Mexico . . ."*

Your body. A wave of nausea washed over James as he realized what was happening. And what he'd done to Mak. He looked at Samuel for answers, but Samuel shook his head, apparently at a loss for words.

"What do you want me to do? Okay, we'll find more details and get back to you. Mak told Kayla she thought he'd be home tomorrow, so we probably won't know much more until then . . . We have a few days at least until the funeral. Okay, talk soon."

There was a brief pause. *"Tomorrow you have to call Mak. Eric wants to know where they found the body and when she's planning to bury him."*

"Why? What is he going to do?"

"I don't know, he didn't say. You can do this, Kayla, you have to."

"I don't want to live this lie anymore."

"That's too bad. Do you think he'll just hurt you, or us? No, he'll go after your entire family and mine. You're going back to work now, and tomorrow you're going to make that call."

There was a long silence, and James thought the phone had been moved out of audible range.

"I'll make the call, and we'll go from there."

"Good. I love you. I'll call you tomorrow."

"Okay, bye."

James heard a rustling noise and assumed Kayla had put the phone back in her handbag.

"Tom. Follow the male. Do not lose him," James said.

"Copy."

The male emerged from the passageway, and James recognized him immediately: he was the coworker in the photographs. The man Mak had run into on the street. The man who had died six years after Eric disappeared.

The man stayed on foot, walking a short distance to an apartment building.

"Tom, secure the building, and do not let him leave. We'll be there soon," James said.

"Copy."

James turned his earpiece off.

"How the fuck did this happen?" James asked, running his hands over his head in frustration.

"Those records weren't tampered with, James. I triple-checked them. The DNA and dental records matched Eric's, even the break in his arm did. And they're old records, they weren't taken just before he disappeared," Samuel said.

James stared at the desk. Slowly, the pieces fell into place. Deacon groaned, and James knew he'd come to the same assumption.

"He planned this," James said. "He planned to disappear years before the first payment was ever made. Someone came to that hospital using his identity, and the same for the dental practice. The film X-ray was a replica of someone else's arm and was planted there. It was all a set up, and we fell for it."

James buried his face in his hands, horrified by the error they'd made.

He'd given Mak the wrong body to bury.

//

ALSO BY BROOKE SIVENDRA

THE JAMES THOMAS SERIES

#1 - ESCANTA

#2 - SARATANI

#3 - SARQUIS

#4 - LUCIAN

#5 - SORIN

#0.5 - THE FAVOR

The complete James Thomas series is available now. THE FAVOR is a novella, and Brooke recommends reading it after SORIN.

THE SOUL SERIES

#1 - The Secrets of Their Souls

#2 - The Ghosts of Their Pasts

#3 - The Blood of Their Sins

A GIFT FROM BROOKE

Brooke is giving away the first book of the Soul Series, *The Secrets of Their Souls*, for **FREE**. All you need to do is sign up here:

http://brookesivendra.com/tsots-download/

Enjoy!

DID YOU ENJOY THIS BOOK?

As a writer, it is critically important to get reviews.

Why?

You probably weigh reviews highly when making a decision whether to try a new author—I definitely do.

So, if you've enjoyed this book and would love to spread the word, I would be so grateful if you could leave an honest review (as short or as long as you like) where you bought it.

Thank you so much,
Brooke

This book is dedicated to my readers.
Thank you for making this journey possible.

ABOUT THE AUTHOR

Brooke Sivendra lives in Adelaide, Australia with her husband and two furry children—Milly, a Rhodesian Ridgeback, and Lara, a massive Great Dane who is fifty pounds heavier than Brooke and thinks she is a lap dog!

Brooke has a degree in Nuclear Medicine and worked in the field of medical research before launching her first business at the age of twenty-six. This business grew to be Australia's premier online shopping directory, and Brooke recently sold it to focus on her writing.

You can connect with Brooke at any of the channels listed below, and she personally responds to every comment and email.

Website: www.brookesivendra.com
Email: brooke@brookesivendra.com
Facebook: http://www.facebook.com/bsivendra
Instagram: http://www.instagram.com/brookesivendra
Twitter: www.twitter.com/brookesivendra

Made in the USA
Middletown, DE
12 April 2018